Hi, My Name Is –

By

Kasha Je'

Copyright © 2022 by Kashina Jegede

First paperback edition November 2022

ISBN 978-1-959941-00-2 (paperback)

ISBN 978-1-959941-01-9 (ebook)

Printed in Maryland, United States of America.

www.kashajebooks.com

I would love to hear from you, reach out to me!

Email: kashajebooks@gmail.com (business inquiries)

Instagram @authorkashaje

Facebook: @kashaJegede-Author

Dedication

I dedicate this book to all young girls who light up any room she walks into with her smile, kindness, brilliance, and full-of-life personality. The girl whose skin is dipped in beautiful shades of brown, and whose heritage covers the globe. The girl whose name is not commonly found on a necklace in a gift shop. The girl whose name is not one or two simple syllables but is enriched by the culture behind it. And to that brave girl who stands up for herself and her friends, and commands the respect of those around her...

I want you to always remember where you come from, who you are, and that self-appreciation is the best gift you can give yourself. Know that you are a magical being and that you are everything!

Kasha

Xoxo

Table of Contents

Foreword

Beautiful Girl,

This story was written just for you in hopes that you learn to embrace what makes you different, accept what makes others different, find and practice self-appreciation, and know and use your superpower of self-discovery to overcome everyday challenges.

Many of us experience our uniqueness as an inconvenience. People mispronounce our names without even trying to get it right. Stores don't carry souvenirs and novelties painted or engraved with names as unique as ours. Some people even try to shrink us down to their comfort level instead of rising to meet us where we are.

Know that being special is part of being the gift that you are. You must always stand up for yourself, even if you have to sacrifice the likes of others.

We are all different in one way or another. Whether it's our accents, our smiles, our facial features, the color of our eyes, the texture of our hair, how tall or short we are, how light or dark our skin is, or how big or small we are...

Just be *you*, first and foremost. Lead with authenticity, rise through bravery, and continue to be unique. Remember, if we were all the same, the world would be a boring place.

Things to remember...

Self-Love – Accepting yourself for who you are and embracing your differences and unique self.

Self-Discovery – Figuring out who you are and developing your identity.

Courage – the willingness and ability to tackle what frightens you.

Chapter One

My Name Is

O yindasola could not believe that she had to start all over again. She clutched her floral leather backpack straps as she walked the same halls of her new middle school that she had been walking for the last hour. At first, she was on the wrong floor. After 20 minutes of peeping in classes, she realized she was on the 9th-grade floor level. A hall monitor guided her to the 8th-grade level below. Why couldn't she find her class? The halls were bare and dull, which seemed to be the total opposite of how an academy would be decorated, but she didn't say anything. At this point, the halls were empty. Another 30 minutes had rolled by when she realized she was walking in circles. "This place is like a maze," she said aloud to no one. She wondered how anybody found anything in the gigantic building. Just as she finished her thoughts, an administrator cleared her throat.

Oyindasola looked up from her schedule to find the source of the sound when she saw a lady with a tight smile waving her over. Oyindasola went to see what this lady wanted from her.

"Do you have a late pass, young lady?"

Oyindasola shook her head. She didn't know where her class was, who the lady was, or why she needed a late pass, considering she had been there well before classes had started.

"Sorry, I'm new here. Can you please tell me where classroom P 108 is? I've been all over this building looking for it." She released a deep exhale. The administrator looked her up and down before sighing and pointing her in the right direction. Finally, Oyindasola could stop endlessly wandering through these never-ending gray and white hallways.

She slowly pried open the old pinewood door and walked into the classroom. The loud screech of the door made all the heads and eyes in the room look at Oyindasola. There were no welcoming smiles or gestures as she crossed the threshold. Instead, everyone just stared in silence. She didn't know what it was. Yes, she had an afro, a very cute one at that. Her stepmom, Shia, says, "*Afros are a part of our culture. They are both bold and adorable,*" She calls them sugar bushes. Had they never seen one before? And yes, there was more melanin in her skin than anybody else combined, but that was no reason for everybody to gawk at her. "Okaaay," she mouthed under her breath.

Finally, the teacher, Mr. Grimsky, snapped out of it and hastily shuffled her into the room. He pointed to the only seat left, a seat in the back corner, and told her to sit. The teacher sighed in annoyance at Oyindasola's tardiness, but she didn't understand.

It was her first day, and she got lost. What was with everyone's demeanor? First, the lady in the hall and now her teacher. While getting settled, she watched as the teacher picked up a thin clipboard to check off her name for attendance.

"We do not tolerate tardiness in my class. So don't make it a habit." Again, he seemed to be disgruntled. He was still looking at his clipboard, but this time with frowned brows. "What is your name so I can take your attendance?"

Oyindasola took a seat in the back corner and put her things under the desk before responding to the teacher's question. "My name is Oyindasola." She answered with her rich accent.

The teacher sighed, and her classmates began to chuckle at her name. She looked around the room. She didn't think anything was funny. That is her name. Her father gave her a name that meant a lot to her. She shrugged her shoulders and took a seat. One kid even began to jeer with his friends about how "exotic" the name Oyindasola was. The teacher even smirked a bit at some of the students' comments before telling them to calm down.

"That's quite a name, and I'm not even trying to pronounce that. Can we call you Shi-Shi or O for short? It would be so much easier for everybody."

Oyindasola took another look around the room. Everybody was looking at her expectantly like she was just supposed to forfeit her name for everybody's convenience. She thought not.

"No," she said emphatically. "My name is Oyindasola. Please address me as so."

The teacher rolls his eyes and marks her present before returning to the lesson. She could feel all the other students' eyes on her. Some even had their mouths open in disbelief that she had told the teacher no, but she paid them no attention as she took down the notes from the board she had missed while trying to find the classroom. Then, she heard the girl sitting beside her loudly scrape her chair across the floor. She moved away from Oyindasola as though she had an incurable disease that the girl didn't want to catch. 'How immature,' she thought. It was disheartening that nobody welcomed her, being that she was the new girl and being treated this way. It definitely was not the welcome she imagined. Did she expect a parade or a party? No, but she expected a little more kindness than what she received. Anyway, this was her name. The teacher asked her, and she gave him her answer. Oyindasola sighed and shrugged her shoulders again. She wanted to make some friends at her new school, but it already seemed like she wouldn't have much luck with that. At least not in this class. After a few moments, the bell rang. All the kids hurried out of the class to tell all their other students about her—the new girl, and how she had a "weird name" and told the teacher he couldn't abbreviate it!

Just as Oyindasola was walking out the door after gathering her things, she felt someone bump her arm. She was shocked and looked up. It was the girl that sat beside her. The one that moved her chair away from her. What did she want? Has the sickness that she thought she would catch earlier worn off now? Before Oyindasola could say anything, the girl slid past her and threw her limp blonde hair over her shoulders.

"You're so pretentious," she snarled. "Why can't you go by a shorter name to make everybody else's life easier? I swear it's always people like you that make it so difficult for people like me to just live." She continued. Oyindasola raised an eyebrow. She was a friendly girl, but she refused to be bullied. "What kind of name is Oyi—Oyindy—uh! Whatever! I swear!" The girl stomped off with her bright pink and orange backpack. Still, Oyindasola couldn't tell if she was already embarrassed or growing tired of everyone's drama. "Why would this girl be upset over the name?" She thought. No one asked her to say it in the first place.

She turned to look through the hallway; everybody was staring at her and pointing. Could this day get any worse? She asked herself. Oyindasola quietly shuffled down the hallway, avoiding eye contact with the laughing and whispering students. She focused more on ensuring she showed up to her next class on time. She was the main attraction on the 8th-grade floor. The start of a sucky first day. As she found her second class, she wiped a bead of sweat that appeared from nowhere as she walked into her second period. Unlike her hopes, it wasn't much better. How was she going to make it through the rest of the day? She wasn't usually like this. Oyindasola was fun and vibrant and liked meeting people, but this school felt overwhelming. Also, she never had a reason to defend her name because back home, everyone had beautiful names like hers, the girls' names, and the boys' names. Also, everyone back home looked and sounded like her as well.

She tried to make the best of it as the first half of the school day started to dwindle. Finally, she was getting the hang of where her classes were. She made sure to stay out of everyone's way, and the second half would be bearable as long as they stayed out of hers.

When the school day was over, and she finally made it home, Oyindasola lay across the middle of her bed and sighed. She replayed the day's events in her head over and over and analyzed bit by bit how her day went. The results? Awful. She walked over to her mirror, took off her navy-blue blazer with Bridgewater Academy embroidered on it, and tossed it on the floor before rolling her eyes at it. She was so nervous and hoped and prayed that today would be a good day, but all she got was mean looks and being teased by the whole class. Even her teacher disliked her!

"I really wanted to make a new friend, but who wants to be friends with a girl like me?" She asked herself out loud while still gazing at herself. "A fine-fine girl like me." She finished while fluffing her afro. But this time, she made herself laugh with a smile and a chuckle. It was the only smile her mouth had made all day. "Can we just call you 'O?'" She mocked her teacher. "What is that?" Her smile turned into anger, and she leaned into the mirror. "No. No, you cannot... Can I call you Mr. Grim?" She laughed again at her wisecrack. "What is a Grimsky anyway?"

If she had to give a review, it would be a one-star, and she would not recommend it. What she hated most was that she had to go back and do it again and again. Could it get any worse than the first day? She questioned. There were still a few more months before the end of the school year.

She remembered years ago when she first met her stepmom, Shia, who is American. "She pronounced my name correctly the first time and effortlessly. I remember her telling me to never let anyone abbreviate my name without my permission and not until they at least try to learn it first." Tomorrow would be another day, and she hoped the other students would be over it so she could be over it too. "I just want to do my work and go home."

After dinner, Shia came to her room to chit-chat like she always did before bedtime. She loved their talks. The two of them had formed a special bond from the moment they met. Whenever she was sad or didn't know what to do, she always went to her first. She always knew what to say, and she always had an answer. She always reminded Oyindasola how brave she was and how important it was to stand her ground and never make herself uncomfortable to satisfy others.

"You have to be brave. Don't let them see you bothered. Bullies prey on the weak. You're not weak. Some kids are mean and hate things they don't understand or haven't been taught. I promise that it has nothing to do with you. So show up tomorrow and show them who you are; a brave, boisterous girl with so much friendship to offer but will take no mess."

Before Shia left the room, she turned around and said,

"Make them put some respect on your name. Period! Okay?" They both laughed as she left the room. But she knew she was being serious. Oyindasola nodded in agreement and replied, "Okay," under her breath. She knew how kids her age could be, but why did it hurt so much? She thought.

Chapter Two

RESPECT

And the next day, she did. Oyindasola walked into her school as if the previous day hadn't happened. She walked in with her head held high and shoulders back with a lot of confidence, her soft afro flowing behind her. It was decorated with an Ankara headband. Her attitude was as if she had been there the whole school year. The girl had a new attitude. "Chin up, Oyin," she coached herself under her breath. She gave her black girl magic a slight tune-up and remembered who she was. Yes, she was friendly, but by no means was she a pushover. She knew that being the new girl would make her a fresh target, but "Not today, and not tomorrow either," she finished.

Oyindasola was exactly where she needed to be and was supposed to be. She insisted that today was a new day, the official first day, and she was going to make the best of it by any means necessary. As soon as she walked into the homeroom, the heads turned, and the whispers started. Some of the boys followed behind her from the hallway, teasing her. "Spoiled Princess, no nickname!" they teased within hearing.

She laughed it off. She thought it was funny. "Boys can be so immature. Sure, I'll be the spoiled Princess, but with my real name," she thought. She was not going to let them dull her mood. She was already loaded. She simply smiled at them and waved from over her shoulder. They looked at each other in confusion. Really? They are giving her a nickname because she didn't want one. So instead of "Shi-Shi" or "O," she is now "Spoiled Princess," which is kind of ironic.

Now, in her homeroom, Oyindasola found and sat in the same seat in the back corner. Taking attendance, Mr. Grimsky looked unexcited as he gave her an exasperated look before he marked her name for attendance. She locked eyes with him and turned up a corner of her mouth, giving him a slight smirk and nodding her head as if to say, "Hello."

All around the room, there were still more jeers about the new girl and the event from the day before, her Princess attitude, and apparent but not so apparent "attention-seeking habits." None of this phased her. None of these kids knew her, so she knew that the kids were just projecting their own feelings onto her. Would she carry their baggage? Absolutely not! As class started, Oyindasola was taking notes from the board when she felt a piece of paper hit the side of her head. She took a deep breath and looked around before picking it up and reading it. It stated, "You're such an attention seeker. First, you won't go by a nickname, and now you are getting all the attention from the boys. You think you're some African Princess or something?"

Oyindasola just smiled and balled the paper up, stuffing it into her backpack. She had envisioned stuffing the balled-up paper into the senders' mouth but decided against it. There was enough satisfaction in her thoughts alone. She adjusted her headband as if it were a crown. She knew the note writer was watching. "It's nothing I can't handle," she reminded herself. She was going to have fun with this and at their expense. At the end of class, she looked for the trashcan so she could toss the note when her eyes locked with an unfamiliar face.

Oyindasola hadn't been at Bridgewater Middle School that long. Still, she recognized everybody who taunted her in first-period homeroom the day before. The girl looked more petite than the rest of her classmates and slightly more ethnic. She gave the girl a slight smile, and the girl smiled back. Then, the girl gave Oyindasola a pitying look before turning back around in her seat and packing the rest of her belongings. Oyindasola was curious about why but decided then and there that girl would be her first friend at Bridgewater. The girl disappeared into the hallway before Oyindasola could approach and speak to her. She tried to catch up, but she was stopped in the hallway by a group of eager and overgrown 8th graders that had heard about her royal highness. They weren't in her classes. But the news got around.

"Hey, Oye, did you guys live in mud huts?" He teased. He was a tall, slinky boy with light brown hair, blue eyes, and crooked teeth.

Then one of his friends chimed in with more uneducated myths about Africa that someone must have misinformed them about. He was also tall, with blue eyes but blonde hair, and he wasn't as skinny as the first boy. They looked way too old and too big to be 8th graders or to be in middle school, but there he was 8th grading.

"Did you guys have clean water?" "What was your pet lion's name?" "Did you have electricity?"

They just kept going on and on with all types of dumb questions. Every uneducated thing they could think of flew from the mouths of those 8th-grade boys. And although they didn't know it, they were pushing her. Oyindasola was shocked because she knew that the boys weren't really interested in or cared about her life back in Nigeria. They just wanted to tease her and act like she was some poor foreigner who had never experienced "American" things. Oyindasola could not stop herself from blowing up in the boys' faces.

She walked up to them very calmly and with a smile on her face. "Lions? Clean water? Mud huts? Where do you think I came from? A jungle? You think you are so funny?" She looked them in the eyes, not waiting for an answer. "Is it because I don't want to be called some dumb nickname? Have you ever considered why?" She continued questioning but waited for no answers. She wasn't interested. She knew that her father had contemplated her name for months. He took his time crafting her name together to form something that was beautiful to him.

Actually, she was okay with a nickname. Everyone has them. She even has one everyone who knows her uses, but she insisted they learned her real name first, respectfully. The two stared back uncomfortably and occasionally looked at each other, not knowing what to say next, even if they wanted to.

"My culture is full of long, boisterous names with colorful spellings with powerful meanings. It's Yoruba." She continued. "YOU don't have to say my name. YOU don't even have to talk to me. But if you want to talk to me, you will learn it." She pointed in their faces. A smile no longer decorated her lips. Their eyes got big as they took a step back.

"Hey, wait!" The crooked-toothed boy was no longer laughing and put up his hands in defeat. He expected her to be intimidated, but she flipped the script on him.

She cut him off... "And no, I've never seen a lion up close or lived in a mud hut. Yes, we have clean water and access to the internet. We have cities just as lively as the ones here in America. We even have our own movie style called Nollywood. I come from a rich culture. As a matter of fact, I never asked for any attention. I don't want to be called 'O' for your convenience. That's it!" she huffed, but she wasn't done. "It's as simple as sounding out syllables. We learned that in elementary school." She sneered.

The two boys looked shocked, as did everybody else who had gathered around them after hearing the commotion. They wanted to put on a show, and she gave it to them, finale, and all. They had not known Oyindasola for a long time, but from what they had heard the day before, they did not think she was the type to blow up like that. The new girl was not the occasional "new quiet girl." She was the new girl who was standing her ground. Before anybody else could say something stupid to Oyindasola, she walked off.

But wait; a voice in her head said, 'finish them,' and she did. "Oh, and by the way," she turned back around and looked at the two boys who were still standing there, speechless and drowning in the laughter of their audience. "The both of you look way too old and too big to be in the 8th grade! And maybe you should visit Nigeria; we have DENTISTS there!" She turned back around and headed down the hallway to her second period. At least this teacher tried to learn her name. All she heard was laughter and clowning from the other students. The tables had turned on those two clowns, and they were now being teased.

Lunchtime rolled around, and the kids were no longer jeering at her, well, at least not the ones who were at the "show" and witnessed her ripping them apart, but word did get around. She had them silenced and was sure she had enough to go around of whatever she was giving out and to whoever needed to get it. They dared not part their lips to tease her at all. Some would look at her and quickly avert their eyes when she caught them looking. She wasn't going to scream or be upset at anybody that was genuinely curious. Still, she made it clear that she would stand up to anyone that tried to bully her.

Once she reached the lunchroom, she was only focused on one thing, finding her newfound friend, who she hoped would become her friend. She spotted the girl sitting alone at a long table and went to sit across from her. Before the girl could speak, Oyindasola stuck her hand out and introduced herself.

"Hi, I saw you in our first-period class, and you were the

only person there who wasn't provoking me. I appreciate that. My name is Oyindasola. What's yours?" She said it slowly so the girl could catch its syllables. The girl seemed shocked by her outgoing personality since it seemed so different from what she saw in class. The girl shook her hand and responded to her question.

"Hi, Oyindasola. My name is Xiuying." She smiled. "Nice to meet you." Oyindasola instantly noticed her accent, and of course, her facial features were a giveaway to where she was from. "I understand what it's like to have a 'not-so-American name.' It took weeks for the teasing to die down about my name, and it felt exhausting. Besides, you seem like a nice person." Xiuying hunched her shoulders.

Oyindasola smiled; she knew that Xiuying looked nice from across the room and was glad she was right. Not only was she friendly, but she said her name effortlessly, and for that, she liked her even more. Although she didn't quite get Xiuying's name correct the first time, she tried again and nailed it the second time. "See, this isn't so hard."

Xiuying and Oyindasola talked nonstop the entire lunch hour about anything and everything. Then, finally, Xiuying asked the question everybody had been dying to ask.

"So why don't you want to go by a nickname? Once I started going by Ying, my life here got much easier."

Oyindasola thought about it and decided to tell her new friend the truth.

"The meaning of my name is a combination of sweetness and wealth in Yoruba. I am a born leader. So it would be the opposite of being brave to buckle under pressure that easily. Growing up, my dad always told me how much time and love he spent creating my name, and others will respect it." She lightly pounded on the table playfully.

From that moment on, Oyindasola would call her new friend Ying when it was just the two of them, but Xiuying when other students were around. Oh, and she gave Ying a nickname to call her as well. It was her middle name, which in fact, is English. Xiuying laughed at all the drama she had caused, but she understood and told her she would only use that name when it was just them.

She was taught that you don't allow people to tell you what they will call you; instead, you tell them what they will call you. Xiuying understood. Her name had a beautiful meaning too, but did she really want to deal with bullies just for that? It wasn't worth it at the time. For that moment, she secretly wished she had met Oyindasola at her moment of weakness or at least had her bravery.

The surrounding students witnessed the two girls' conversation and saw how much they enjoyed each other's company. Seeing the duo mentally shifted their mindset. Why was there a problem with the new girl to begin with? Oyindasola wasn't the problem; maybe they were. Some of them had names that were not the simplest, but their names didn't have a deep or cool meaning.

Oyindasola didn't know it yet, but the mindsets of her bullies were starting to shift. She was one of the few brown students on the 8th-grade floor, but the entire school was diverse, so she didn't understand the big deal. But today, she has broken ground.

Chapter Three

Mirror, Mirror

T here was so much Oyindasola still couldn't figure out about Bridgewater Academy. It was clear who the majority were at this school, and it became more noticeable to her the more she got familiar. One thing she started to notice was that she was the only African student on her grade floor. There were some black American students, but she was the only African.

As she got more comfortable with Bridgewater and its people, she couldn't help but notice how friendly some students were to the American students who looked like her. Some of the African American girls were dark brown, just like her, so maybe the students weren't discriminating against her. Perhaps it was her? Was she the problem?

On that Friday afternoon, she still noticed the difference in how she was treated compared to the other brown-skinned girls, or so she thought. They were all the same to Oyindasola. Were they more accepted than her because they were born here? Or even a better type? Whatever that could mean. When Oyindasola saw Xiuying talking to some of the black American girls while passing in the hallway, she really felt it. What did they have that she didn't? The only difference she noticed was that her skin tone was darker.

When she got home from school, she rushed upstairs into her room to gather her thoughts. This whole new school transition was making her a wreck. After barging up the stairs and shaking the house with the loud rumblings through the hallways, Oyindasola's sister decided to go and see what the big deal was, and maybe she could help. Ava was not at all expecting what she saw. She was sitting at her desk chair with her phone in one hand while trying to wipe her tears away with the other hand. What was wrong with Oyindasola? Ava rushed over to check on her little sister. Middle school is rough for anybody, especially those new to the country and its people. Ava reached out and put a hand on Oyindasola's shoulder before turning to hug her sister.

"What's wrong?"

Oyindasola didn't even know what to tell her sister. This new start had all her emotions attacking her at once. She didn't know what to make of it. She hated that she had to fight to exist and wondered how long she would have to keep defending herself over something so ridiculous. Why was it so hard for her to make new friends although she now had Xiuying. What was she upset over, and with whom? Is she expecting too much, too soon? Why did she envy seeing Xiuying with other friends? She had never talked to the African American girls she envied, so she shouldn't be mad at them, but Oyindasola couldn't help it. She was just so jealous of the other brown girls. Why couldn't she be like them? Did she think they were making more friends because she thought they were prettier? Was she now being a spoiled Princess? Maybe if she talked like them and let people call her by her nickname, people would start to talk to her. She can't drop her accent; she was born with it.

Oyindasola's mind was racing with all sorts of questions and thoughts, whether they made sense or not, until her sister finally told her to just let it all out. And she did. She told her older sister everything about her new school. The bullying, the

African American girls, her friend Xiuying, about wanting to be herself but still wanting to fit in, and finally, noticing that she is the darkest brown girl in the 8th grade. She told her big sister absolutely everything.

After all she had said, Oyindasola felt a huge weight lift off her shoulders, so much so that she let out a deep sigh. Ava took a deep breath and thought about everything her sister had told her. She was also a new high school student, but her luck with fitting in was not a problem. She was lucky enough to have met other students from Nigeria and those who weren't were interested in knowing more about her and her home. Ava sat near her on the bed before giving her some advice.

"Listen, sometimes it's hard being the new kid. It feels like nobody knows or likes you, and nobody wants to. Everyone is not going to be your friend, and that's okay. Plus, you started in the middle of the school year, so not only are you new, but you are "new-new," but I promise it will get better. There is nothing wrong with your skin. You might be the only African girl in the 8th grade, but you're not the only black or brown girl there. We come in all shades of beautiful brown tones. You already know this too. So why do you put yourself down for something that you love and admire in others? It makes no sense. Because everyone is not flocking to be your friend, you think you're ugly? Abeg!" Ava rolled her eyes.

"My hair looks bad; I'm so dark, I don't look like other black girls. No wonder the kids at school don't talk to me."

It was criticism after criticism before her sister finally just yelled, "Stop!" There was so much for her to tell her little sister, who had suddenly become so insecure. This behavior was not her at all.

"You have beautiful brown skin. Who cares if it is darker than the other girls? Beauty comes in all shades, not just lighter-skin tones. You shouldn't see the other brown girls as competition. You resent people you never met when they have done nothing to you. I advise you to recognize the other black girls as genuine people just trying to survive at Bridgewater Academy, just like you. Besides, you just started, and they've been there for who knows how long. Nobody walks in the door with people flocking to them to be friends. There is absolutely nothing about yourself that you could or should change to gain the acceptance of the other students. You are who you are. You need to love and accept yourself as you did before you started that school. Promise that you won't try to change the unchangeable. Your name is O-yin-da-sola, and you are African girl magic." She snapped her fingers and chuckled. Their stepmom would say that to them, followed by a finger snap to give it some attitude

Oyindasola hadn't even thought about what her sister said before now, and she was right. You can't change your skin color; even if she could, she knew she wouldn't want to. She looked at her dark-skinned sister and thought about her dark-skinned parent. She thought they were all beautiful people inside and out. If she didn't like her dark skin, did that mean she didn't like her family members' skin? She didn't even want to entertain the thought of that. Back home in Nigeria, people come in all shades of brown, so what was the deal? She was now confused by her thoughts and feelings and realized she was just making up stuff.

"I promise." She agreed.

Her sister shook her head with a smile before reaching over to fluff Oyindasola's big, yummy afro. "And you love sugar bushes, but if you wanted your hair done in another style, all you had to do was ask. Come on; I'll do it." And her big sister did.

She sat on the floor on a pillow and turned on a movie while her sister began parting her hair into small chunks.

As she got ready for bed, her Shia came in to say good night. Ava had already told her what was going on.

"Hey, Cutie Pie," she greeted while Oyindasola was wrapping her freshly braided hair with a scarf. She always called her by some sweet little nickname. "I know how you feel, and I know you already know what I'm going to say but believe me when I tell you and when everyone tells you that you are beautiful. Girl! Look in the mirror. You are so lucky to have been blessed with smooth chocolate brown skin. Everyone loves chocolate. She teased. And your skin is flawless. And yes, your afro really is fly. Snap out of it, Buttercup, and get out of your own head. Have you ever thought of it this way…? Maybe, just maybe, as much as you are intimidated by them, those same girls are intimidated by you. For all you know, they could be saying, 'Wow, look how beautiful she is. I wish I could wear my hair like that!' Yep, they could be thinking the same thing as you. But one thing is certain: you can't be beautiful and treat yourself like an ugly person. That just doesn't add up. Go to school tomorrow, be that fun-loving girl who loves everybody, and walk up to your new friends and say, 'Hi, my name is... What's yours?'"

———————————————

She texted her two closest friends back home in Nigeria, whom she hadn't chatted with in at least a week. However, they kept in touch as often as possible while keeping up with the time differences. She sent an 'eye rolling' gif in the latest group chat. Almost immediately, Adaego responded with a 'confused look' gif, and Ifunanya sent a bunch of question marks.

Oyin: I miss you guys!!!!

Nanya: We miss you too Shira!

Dae: How is school there? Have you made friends yet?? You betta not replace us now.

Nanya: She can't replace us Dae. We are the ORIGINALS!!!!!

Oyin: School can be better. I did meet a friend she's Chinese. The only one who's been nice to me. In this school, do you know I am the ONLY African gyal in my grade. It's so much nonsense I put up with in just my few days there.

Nanya: only one???

Nanya: Only u????

Dae: Wetin?

Oyin: 2 days, 2 days. I tell you, I had to put some people in check. They thought they would bully me oh! Cause im dey new gyal. I won't have it.

Dae: abeg!! Don't put up with dat rubbish

Oyindasola loved talking to her closest girls. They had all gone to the same school since elementary years. She missed her full life in Nigeria, liked her new home in America but disliked her school. They chatted for the remaining hour until Adaego and Ifunanya had to go, as they were 5 hours ahead in time and it was getting late.

On the following school day, Oyindasola tried to have a different outlook on the situation. Everybody was trying to survive middle school; everybody had had their first day and new kid blues, and she would not resent them for that. When Oyindasola saw Xiuying the next school day, she grabbed her hand and made a very important request.

"Can you introduce me to the girls that you were talking to on Friday?"

Xiuying was ecstatic and dragged her in the opposite direction to meet her other friends. She was excited for all of her friends to get to know each other so they could all hang out together in one group. Oyindasola was a bit nervous about meeting more new people, especially since the previous drama. Still, as they got closer to the group of two African American girls and an Indian girl, who had welcomed her presence with a smile, she felt more comfortable. Xiuying excitedly introduced Oyindasola, and the girls smiled and introduced themselves.

"I'm Aaliyah."

"I'm Jada."

"I'm Imani."

The girls seemed really friendly.

"Hi, I'm Oyindasola." Finally, she relaxed and introduced herself. "Nice to meet you."

"We know who you are," Jada grinned, with a raised brow. You're the new girl who is making everybody get her name right! Good for you." Aaliyah, Imani, and Jada teased while giving her a high five. The girls smiled and swept both she and Xiuying into their conversation. Oyindasola was so happy she didn't know what to do.

"By the way, I loved your afro; it was really dope," Imani said. "Yes! But your braids are really cute. Who did them?" asked Aaliyah. "My sister," she answered with a humbled smile.

Her big sister was right. The right people would accept you just how you are, and her stepmom was right. She was in her own head, and they liked her the whole time.

Chapter Four

Culture Day

I t was a cool, breezy Monday morning heading to Bridgewater Academy. Oyindasola sat in World Geography class with the rest of her mates, chatting until the teacher was ready to start class. The room was as loud and happy as it usually is, but today, class felt different.

She observed the room, trying to figure out why the day felt so happy and upbeat when Ms. Portly, the teacher, welcomed her students to a new week, as she did every week, and began to introduce the next assignment. An orchestra of sighs, moans, and groans sent a wave across the room as some students loudly complained about more homework. But they were wrong this time. "Nooo, it's not homework," she laughed at them. "More like a project," she clarified. The class cheered up again. It seems everyone prefers projects over homework.

"Project?" *Oyindasola* thought. What was the project about? She didn't have to wait to learn about the project because Ms. Portly started to explain it right away.

"Students, let me have your attention." She returned the focus back to her and her announcement. "We, or should I say you, are going to be doing a project on different countries and cultures worldwide."

"Oh, this is going to be fun!" one student exclaimed happily from his seat. She continued. "You can choose any country, in any place in the world. Whether it be France with its culture of art and delicate desserts or Brazil with its culture of Carnival and indigenous-Portuguese fusion. There are nearly 200 countries in the entire world, so branch out and learn about something you don't know too much about and teach us something new. Try to pick a place we rarely hear about," she continued. "You can choose a culture you are a part of or one that looks interesting. You will make a poster board with information about the country, its culture, language, and any important history. Since we will be in a time crunch and there are 17 of you, you will only get 7 minutes to present. Learning about diversity and culture is the whole point of this project, so put in all your creative energy and teach us something." The whole class was filled with excitement as all the students discussed which countries they should choose. "Oh, and one more thing; this project is due this Friday." She smiled and quickly turned her back to them. "Friday?!"

They all complained but laughed at her shenanigans. Ms. Portly always did things like that to them, but her spontaneity was the one thing that made her class fun and her a fun teacher. You never knew what she was going to spring on you. She continued chuckling at them. "You will present the project to the class. Although you are not required to, you will receive extra credit for extra efforts, like attire, handouts, foods, and activities that represent the culture. Some of you need the extra credit, so think outside the box." "Ooooh." The class roared and snickered at her snippy remark. "So if you were presenting France, you could bring in macaroons, for example. Are there any questions, comments, or concerns about this project? Speak now or forever hold your peace."

Everyone understood the assignment and continued chatting about it excitedly, and they began working on their ideas. Oyindasola and Xiuying looked at each other with huge smiles. This was something they could do with ease. Since they both struggled with the same thing with their classmates being the "odd" foreigners, they knew that a culture and diversity project would put the ball in their court. This was going to be so much fun and an easy A for sure.

Oyindasola couldn't believe that she would get to talk about Nigeria and her Yoruba culture, and the other kids had to listen. She planned to introduce exciting and cool facts about how incredible her culture is. Oyindasola was pleased. As she was packing up, Xiuying tapped her shoulder with a smile. She was just as happy with the project as her bestie was.

"Hey, Oyindasola. Aren't you excited? I'm so excited. This is going to be so much fun for us. As diverse as this school is, some kids have no idea just how interesting culture and identity can be."

Oyindasola picked up her things, and she and Xiuying walked towards the door. "Exactly! It's like they have no idea what they are missing out on. I have the perfect surprise to add for extra credit. My dad recently returned from Nigeria and brought home a bunch of coconut candies!"

Xiuying smiled and shook her head at her happy friend. This was going to be good for them. As the two best friends walked from Geography to Math, Xiuying got an idea. A sleepover. That's it. So not only could the class learn about each culture better, but she and Oyindasola could actually get up close to each other's culture. Who wouldn't want to have a sleepover with their newly found best friend?

That afternoon, Oyindasola suddenly felt a happy tug on her arm. She spun around and was met with a once again excited Xiuying. "What's up? Why do you look so happy all of a sudden? I mean, you were happy all morning, but now you seem way happier." Xiuying smiled and pulled her off to the side of the hallway so they could talk.

Oyindasola thought it was a great idea. She hadn't gotten a real chance to hang with Xiuying outside of school, and she knew that her dad would say yes. The two agreed and continued on their way to Math class. After a quick text to their parents to make sure it was okay, the girls scheduled a dinner date for Friday night and a sleepover.

When Oyindasola arrived home, she told her dad and stepmom about her day. She greeted them with a much bigger smile than usual after a day at school. So, they knew something good was brewing for her, and they would hear all about it. Everything from the class project to dinner at Xiuying's to the plantains she was anxious to share with her class for Friday. Oyindasola's dad could do nothing but chuckle at his daughter. He loved that she was excited about sharing her culture.

She spoke a mile a minute, trying to get out everything that had happened that day. She spoke so fast that some of her words were not even in English but in her Yoruba dialect, and she didn't even realize it until he pointed it out. The excitement of it all had her speaking two languages at once.

He was also pleased that Bridgewater took the time to recognize other places and their cultures. He knew that she had been having a tough time getting adjusted and blending in with her identity. Sometimes people in America forget that other countries are beautiful with wonderful traditions, practices, and beliefs and that a good chunk of America is populated with different cultures from across the water. Oyindasola had a lot to learn about her Yoruba culture, and he was more than happy to teach her a few facts to share with her class.

"Come sit with me. Let me tell you some facts about Nigeria and our people, the Yorubas." He pats the spot on the sofa next to him. She hurriedly plopped down next to him, notebook and pen in hand. "Even I cannot tell you all our history and traditions, but give me a couple of minutes, and your project will be the easiest thing you have ever done."

And that's exactly what Oyindasola 's father did. He spoke of the Nigerian independence from Britain in the 1960s, which he had learned in school and through his parents, and facts about their tribe, one of Nigeria's three largest ethnic groups. He told her what the colors of the Nigerian flag meant. He went on and on about mythology and more history, but she planned on making this fun, and this was her moment to shine.

She listened to him but only took the meat and threw away the bone. Which meant she only kept the parts she was interested in sharing. He reminded her to show them the Gele, the elegantly styled headdresses, and Iros and Buba, the beautifully vibrant dresses worn by girls and women. By the time Oyindasola's father was done speaking, she felt as though she had a completely new outlook on Nigeria and who she and her people were. She lived in the present, but the past was a whole other world. It was beautiful.

Oyindasola reached out her arms to her dad and gave him a huge hug. He was always there to help and guide her whenever she needed him. And he never judged her or pushed her to be something she wasn't. He simply provided insight, wisdom, and support. Besides, he loved talking about home because he is a proud Nigerian. From Tuesday to Friday, Oyindasola's big sister Ava and stepmom eagerly assisted her with her presentation. They knew how important this was to her. They got a huge poster board and decorated it in the colors of the Nigerian flag. Her stepmom cooked plantains, and her dad fried up cow beans to make chin-chin. Her father ensured the history was accurate and that all the essential details were on the poster board.

The night before, Oyindasola's sister styled her beautiful braids and looked over her presentation once more for her. Everything was coming together perfectly. On that Friday morning, Oyindasola woke up, showered, and dressed in her special attire for the day—a purple, red, and gold printed Gele swirled into a beautiful design and an Iro and Buba. She made sure to pack her uniform to change after class. She looked over herself one last time in the mirror and repeated her morning affirmations before leaving.

"I am beautiful."

"I am magical."

"I am brave."

"I can't be stopped."

"My name is Oyindasola."

Oyindasola's family thought she looked stunning. The braids sat perfectly on her shoulders, and the clothing lay elegantly. She picked up her backpack and the bag of goodies for her presentation, which included coconut candy, chin-chin, and a bowl of sweet plantains. Finally, she was ready for school. She made a mental note to take some of the candy out to stash in her locker for herself.

When Oyindasola walked into Bridgewater Academy that Friday morning, it was like the world had stopped. Her walk from the car to the school's front door to her class felt like a runway. Everybody, from teachers to students to parents, stopped to admire the beauty of her traditional African attire. Comments of "beautiful," "wow," and "cool" surrounded her as she walked to class. Other students dressed the part, but it was nothing like hers. Finally, she spotted Xiuying, and she looked beautiful as well. Xiuying was decked out in a beautiful green, gold, and white Qipao adorned with red and pink flowers, and Ji sticks accessorized her hair. She looked amazing and still looked extremely happy. Oyindasola realized that Ying needed this much more than she did. At this moment, wearing her culture's clothing and holding her culture's food was where she was her absolute happiest.

Oyindasola was content. They immediately stopped to snap photos of each other and to take selfies, of course. The two friends sat through several mundane classes before it was finally time for the big moment. Everybody piled into the World Geography class and quickly found their seats. The class smelled amazing; the posters were colorful, and there were accessories everywhere.

The teacher walked down the aisles of desks, having each student pick a number from a little box. This is the number that each student had to present. Of course, there were 17 kids in the class, and Oyindasola got the 17th. Xiuying said that they must have saved the best for last. She was so funny. She smiled, thinking how good of a friend Xiuying had to be to say that to her.

The presentations started, and they were kind of cool, but one thing was clear; a few of the kids picked very similar countries that were obvious. She thought, "How lucky am I to be from another country?" Most of her class was American-born, and they all picked the obvious Western European countries, so there were several repeats. How lazy of them. There were quite a few berets in the crowd and two big trays of croissants with preserves and butter. Although he was born here, one of the boys presented France, where his parents are from. His presentation on France was the best of all the others in that area of Europe. The funny part is that he brought french fries! But as a joke, of course. Ms. Portly side-eyed him, but she thought it was funny too.

A few other countries were also represented, like Mexico, Ireland, Thailand, and Australia.

Besides a few more good things, Oyindasola and Xiuying would show them just how interesting the rest of the world was. While most of the class presented what they've learned in school or found in the library, they got to report on something of their own. Their world. Then it was Xiuying's turn. She was number 16 and ready to show the class her beautiful Chinese culture.

"Ni Hao… Hi everyone. My name is Xiuying, but you all call me 'Ying' for short. My project is about the People's Republic of China. China is a huge country, just a bit larger than the United States. There are 56 different ethnic groups, and I am from the most common one—Han. China is known throughout the world for its beautiful red and gold lanterns for Lunar New Year and its beautiful clothing, such as Qipao and Ji sticks, like what I am wearing right now." She twirled and continued, "I brought in traditional snacks for everyone to try, and no, it's not egg rolls and fortune cookies." She teased. Everyone, including Ms. Portly, laughed.

"I have Bingtang-Hulu and White Rabbit candy." She finished by explaining what they were.

Oyindasola and the rest of the class were so interested in everything Xiuying said that they forgot about the snacks. Well, some of them. Some were only waiting for everyone's presentation to end so the snacks could be passed around. When Xiuying finished, the whole class erupted in cheers.

Oyindasola was the loudest one, obviously supporting her best friend. It was beautiful. A class of happy, cheerful, and educated people was arising. Besides, it made Xiuying feel good, and her best friend could see that.

Oyindasola was next. Xiuying hi-fived her as if she was tagging her in for a battle. She stood up and dragged her poster board to the front of the room. "Bawo Ni," waving her hand hello. She opened her board and turned it towards the class. There were "oohs" and "ahhs" from the class when they saw the vibrant green and white poster. She even had attached small samples of other vibrant fabric patterns like the one she had on. This was off to a great start.

Just like Xiuying, Oyindasola explained the origins of her clothing, the Yoruba culture, and the most popular food. "Wow, you're from a tribe?" One of the classmates asked in disbelief. She thought tribes only existed in movies. She explained Nigeria's independence from the British in 1960 and that the green and white flag colors represented wealth and peace. She also shared that one of her favorite dishes was Jollof rice, Egusi soup, and plantain. She taught them to say, "Hi, my name is..." She had each classmate say "Hi, oruko mi ni" and their name. Some had to do it twice, but they got it right. Even the kids who didn't like it got it, although they pretended not to be interested. They really were. Her best friend was next. She eagerly stood up, "Hi, oruko mi ni Xiuying." The two giggled at each other. Xiuying could be extra sometimes, and they both knew it. She even had Ms. Portly say it as well.

Everyone listened intently when Oyindasola was speaking, but they paid special attention when she talked about the big tray of delicious-smelling plantains that sat in the front of the room. However, before Oyindasola finished her presentation, she had one last thing to do.

"Lastly, I will tell you how to pronounce my name. It is O-yin-dah-sola. Sound it out with me, 'O-yin-dah-sola.'" She also had that pronunciation attached to her board as well. "O-yin-dah-sola," they repeated. "Thank you!" The meaning of my name is a combination of sweetness and wealth." Almost everyone gasped, and even Ms. Portly was in awe. "In case you didn't know, a name is also a part of someone's culture. Our names are our identities and, in most cases, will tell you where a person is from. It is who we are. If you can't pronounce someone's name or even take the time to try, you don't really care about or respect that person as a human worthy of identity. I appreciate your attention during my project on Nigeria and my Yoruba culture. I brought Plantain and Coconut candies to share."

Another loud round of applause from her class, and she even heard a few people say her name as she walked back to her seat. She and Xiuying squealed. They did it! They absolutely crushed their projects and were so happy that they chose their own cultures and that everybody else seemed genuinely interested. With the project in the bag and the class breaking open the plantains, croissants, chin-chin, french fries, coconut candy, and all the other snacks in the room, Xiuying and Oyindasola locked arms. An unspoken victory had been had.

After World Geography, the girls left for the hall when a few classmates stopped them. "Oyin-dasola!" She heard her name a few times, catching her off guard. She quickly turned around to meet two boys and two girls who had given her trouble on the first day. One of the girls was the one who had slid her chair away from her and had also written her that ugly note. Shocked that they said her name... "What's up?" she asked with raised brows. Finally, one boy spoke up first. "I just wanted to say I'm sorry for giving you such a hard time on your first day and calling you a spoiled Princess. Your name is pretty, and the meaning is really like... wow," he exclaimed with a slight blush.

The other two followed up with apologies as well. That made Oyindasola smile. But note girl was still giving stank attitude energy. She continued to pass them, rolling her eyes at Oyindasola and mean-mugging the guys. Ironically, her sidekick changed her smile to an emotionless look and walked off with note girl. She knew that her loyalty was to her friend. That made Oyindasola smile too. There was no love lost, anyway, back to the duo. It wasn't that they disliked her; they just thought she was trying to be extra dramatic by not using a nickname. Even people with easy names had short nicknames.

"Your presentation was amazing. "The guys almost said in unison." "And so was yours too," Aiden, the French fry guy, said to Xiuying, but he was still smiling at her, Oyindasola.

"Thank you." The besties sang in unison with giggles.

"I appreciate it, guys. But now I have to tell you something." She covered her chuckle with her arm.

"Yea?" they quizzed.

"I do have a nickname." She laughed some more.

The five of them stood there dumbfounded with their mouths open in disbelief.

"You can now call me Amelia if you like. It's my English name." She smiled at Aiden.

"Wait, you went through all that and had a nickname the whole time?" The note girl asked with her sidekick standing next to her at the lockers across the hall.

She was ear-hustling and wanted to know everything Aiden was saying to her. It was no secret she liked Aiden, and the fact that she had been there the entire year and here comes this new girl stealing his attention did not sit right with her.

"Yes, everyone seemed to have judged me the moment I walked through the door and insisted that I should answer by whatever name you chose for me without even trying."

Aiden and his friend nodded their heads in agreement. The four of them stood there conversing while the note girl was still across the hall, throwing all the shade and attitude she

Hi, My Name Is —

could while venting to her friend and slamming her lockers door. Note girl's friend didn't seem to have a problem with Oyindasola. She had given her a slight smile as they walked off down the hall, but of course, behind the note girl's back.

The four of them kinda laughed at her behavior. "What is with her?" Oyindasola asked but not waiting or caring for an answer.

"Anyway, I want to go and change she told Xiuying. I'll meet you in the bathroom. I need to stop at my locker first." As beautiful as her Ankara attire was, she did want to wear the stiff fabric any longer than she had to. Although a part of her wanted to leave on the full attire to collect a few more eye rolls from 'the jel squad.' That's what she and her friends called jealous girls in school back home.

Down the hall, around the corner, Oyindasola pulled her bag from her locker and headed back to the bathroom. She was in a good mood but couldn't control her smile when she saw that Aiden was still standing in the same space as they were before, right outside World Geography. She caught him stealing looks when he thought she wasn't watching. She thought it was sweet that he had an obvious crush on her, but he was doing a bit much now. She avoided eye contact with him and continued to the bathroom, a few doors down.

Once in the bathroom, Oyindasola made her way to Xiuing, who was getting her clothes laid out. They had yet to speak a word when the bathroom door opened on the other side of the lockers. They overheard the voice of the note girl and her friend talking about her, which made her and Ying remain quiet and listen in.

She ranted on about how long she had been at Bridgewater and how Aiden hadn't chosen her to be his girlfriend yet... blah blah blah. She then started to mention Oyindasola. That's when both girls really tuned in, staring directly into each other's eyes, wondering what they would hear.

"This Oyi girl is getting on my nerves, and she just got here, and she has the whole floor talking about her." Note girl fumed. "Who does this girl thinks she is? African, yes, but Princess, no!" Aiden was teasing her with the rest of us not too long ago, and now he can't stop smiling every time he sees her." Her ranting continued as she stopped pacing back and forth, finally resting on one of the sinks. Oyindasola and Xiuying silently chuckled at note girls' rants, covering their mouths tightly to not release a sound.

"Why are you so nice to her anyway?" note girl questioned her quiet friend, who just sat on the bench listening to her endless rants. "You were right along with me and the others when she rolled in here on her high horse—I mean jungle lion." Note girl and her friend laughed.

"Honestly, Alaina, yes, I was laughing and being an idiot with everyone else, but truthfully, I like her name, and I like her. The girl has not bothered or even looked in your direction. Is it that you don't like that she prefers to be called by her name or that Aiden likes her when you like him? Why does Oyinso—Oyindaso—bother you so much? Oyindasola chuckled again at the mispronunciation but liked that she tried to get it right. Sidekick friend continued, "The girl bothers nobody. You can't be mad at her for setting boundaries for herself. Also, you must admit, her presentation was good" She shrugged her shoulders matter-of-factly.

Alaina just rolled her eyes at her friend, and she wasn't letting up. She slowly realized that when Aiden was teasing Oyindasola, it wasn't the same as her teasing. He actually liked Oyindasola, and for that, Alaina felt foolish, making her even more upset that she and Aiden were not on the same side.

"Whose side are you on anyway, Natalia? Are you my friend or not? Where is the loyalty?" Of course, I'm your friend, and that means telling you when you're wrong. I'm just trying to get you off her back. Besides, if you were the new girl, would you want people treating you the same way?" Natalia questioned Alaina and stared at her, waiting for an answer.

"Well, she needs to go back where she came from. She just got here, and she's already doing way too much. So as long as she stays here, I'm going to—"

"To do what?" Oyindasola finally appeared from behind the locker, with Xiuying following behind her. She was over this girl and her attitude. The look on Alaina's face was priceless. She didn't know Oyindasola was there the entire time.

"Girl, what are you talking about?" Alaina questioned dumbfoundedly.

"Finish your threat. So as long as she stays here, I'm going to…what?" Oyindasola waited for her to answer. Alaina shooed her hand away towards the duo and rolled her eyes.

"I'm not scared of you, 'Princess.'" She put her finger up in quotations.

"You don't have to be scared, but you are jealous." The "j" word triggered Alaina. Xiuying laughed. "Shut up, Ying!" Alaina spatted. Angry herself for her embarrassment. Ying covered her mouth but continued smiling.

She looked over at Natalia, who was still sitting but tuning in.

"I'm not your issue. You are!"

Oyindasola raised her voice and pointed. "And if this helps you feel any better, I don't want Aiden, but news flash, HE doesn't want YOU either!" she pointed again. This time Natalia had a slight smile on her face. She was secretly pleased that Oyindasola was putting Alaina in her place. So many girls at that school didn't. She was intimidating, not because of her height, voice tone, or bite but because of her mean girl complex; however, once you challenged her, you realized she was all bark and no bite. Alaina stepped closer to her. Oyindasola was not a fighter. She never thought it was necessary, but if Alaina even tried her at that moment, she promised an unscripted reality show beatdown, imported all the way from the Motherland.

Xiuying was having a time with this. Her smirk never left her face. Alaina was one of the students who had also given her so much trouble because of her name, which made her eventually go with 'Ying.' She was loving this. She had heard about the guys that Oyindasola had handled previously through hallway chitter chatter, and now she was witnessing this for herself.

"You don't know what Aiden likes—"

"Alaina, let's go. This is silly now."

"Ughh! shut up, Natty." She spat in an annoying tone. She was tired of hearing how Aiden wasn't into her.

"It's Natalia." She sternly looked into her eyes, correcting Alaina. She was friends with Alaina, but her spoiled girl demeanor allowed her to take things too far. Natalia was growing tired of the disrespect towards her and others. She started to question if Alaina really saw her as a friend. The funny thing is Alaina has never called her 'Natty.' Not ever. Natalia said what she said, stood, and walked towards the bathroom door. She looked back at Oyindasola... "It's not worth it. I promise she doesn't bite," she offered and walked out.

Alaina didn't quite realize it at that moment, but she had lost a friend. One of the few girls in the 8th-grade that would tolerate her. Natalia was tired of being treated like her sidekick. Now, realizing she was in that space alone with the trouble she had stirred up, she took a step back. Oyindasola took Natalia's advice and walked back to the locker room to finish changing out of her Ankara attire. She didn't look back or utter another word. Alaina, further embarrassed, quietly left the bathroom. The girls only realized she had left after hearing the door open and then close. Then they roared with laughter.

"Well done, best friend, well done!" Xiuying cheered, offered a high five, and finished it with a dance move that Oyindasola couldn't quite recognize. But, of course, that made her laugh even more.

The girls retreated into the hall when they saw the guys still talking. The guys swept them up into their conversation until the last bell of the day rang, and they all said their goodbyes and dispersed.

"See you around, Oyindasola-Amelia." Aiden walked away with another smile.

"Ooooh..." Ying teased.

"Dake Ying!" She walked off quickly, trying to hide her smile. "Did you just tell me to shut up?" Ying followed, still teasing her.

Next stop, dinner at Ying's house, and then a sleepover.

Chapter Five

Duck, Anyone?

Immediately after the last bell rang, Amelia and Ying piled into Mrs. Chen's car. The car smelled like ginger and vanilla and was cool, but Amelia paid it no mind as she gushed to Ying about how excited she was for the dinner and the sleepover that would take place at her house later. Amelia did not forget her manners. She spoke to Ying's mom as soon as she got in the car.

"Ni Hao, Mrs. Chen"

"Oh, I see my daughter has been teaching you. Good job." She nodded with a friendly smile.

"I'm Amelia. I am really excited about dinner. Thanks for having me. It means a lot. "

"It's a pleasure, Amelia. How kind of you."

Mrs. Chen smiled at Amelia's excitement. She was happy that her daughter had found a friend. Ying talked about her all the time, and now she finally got to meet this newfound bestie from Nigeria. She and her husband, Mr. Chen, loved the fact that their daughter was able to make friends from other cultures and have always wanted her to have a diverse circle. Amelia smiled. She was grateful that Ying's parents had allowed her to have dinner with them.

"It's nice to finally meet you, Amelia." Mrs. Chen responded, looking at her in the rearview mirror. "Ying has told me so much about you. Mr. Chen is at home finishing dinner and setting up the table."

Oyindasola smiled to herself at the mention of Mr. Chen cooking. She thought of her dad, who was always in the kitchen when it was time for some good traditional meals.

"We're having Peking duck and scallion pancakes. They are some traditional Chinese dishes since Xiuying told me about your school's culture day."

Amelia thought that sounded delicious and couldn't wait to try it. When they got to the Chen family home, it was quaint and beautiful. The house was a Victorian home. The two girls grabbed their bags and rushed into the house. They could smell dinner as soon as they approached the front door. Once inside, they were met by a smiling Mr. Chen.

"Well, hello, girls."

"Hi, Papa!" Ying greeted her dad before hugging his neck.
"Hi, Mr. Chen." Amelia nodded her head to greet him.

"Nǐ Hǎo, Oyindasola is your name, isn't it? I want to get it
right." He teased, pointing at her. Remembering his daughter's
story about what happened in class some time ago.

"Nǐ Hǎo, and yes, you said it perfectly." Amelia greeted
him again and was tickled at how Ying's parents already knew
her name and made an effort to pronounce it correctly. It felt
good to have other adults outside her parents put in an effort
to say her name.

"My traditional name is Oyindasola, but my English name
is Amelia. You can call me either one." She added.

"Well, thank you, Amelia." Mr. Chen smiled and sent the girls
off to settle and wash their hands before dinner. The girls went
up the stairs and into Ying's room to relax until dinner was ready.

Amelia loved how beautifully decorated Ying's room was.
Her furniture was minimal, but the decorations on her wall
were a mixture of traditional Chinese art and posters of her
favorite K-Pop artists.

"This is your room? It's so cool. Oh, look at the dragon. That's really cool. Where did you get that?"

Ying picked up the stuffed dragon that Amelia was fawning over and hugged it tightly.

"It's from Beijing. I got it when I was 3, and it's been with me. Dragons are a huge part of Chinese mythology, and it's fascinating to learn about them. Her name is Heng, which means eternal in Mandarin."

While getting settled, they would talk about the event in the locker room with Alaina and Natalia. Ying thought there was going to be a fight. She had seen a side of her friend that she didn't expect. It was the bravery that Amelia possessed that Ying admired her for. Amelia didn't know, but she was teaching Ying without actually teaching her; Ying was definitely taking notes. "I wasn't going to fight, well, at least I didn't want to. And fight for what? She doesn't like me because someone I don't like—likes me, and she likes him, and because she doesn't like that I stand up for myself. I've already one."

Ying's eyes grew big. "I thought you were going to hit her at one point." I don't care to fight. I got too much to lose, and it's not worth it. But I had to let her know that if provoked, she could get these hands. Period! I will walk away from a fight, but I will not be bullied."

Ying then looked at her with a cheeky smile and raised eyebrows. "Don't you dare mention Aiden!" Amelia warned through a slight smile. She knew now that Aiden liked her for sure, and she kind of thought he was friendly and cute, but she was not into him. Besides, she knew she wasn't allowed to date, so there was that.

"You can't deny that he's kinda cute, though."

"Hmmm, yea, he's okay. Okay, yea, he is cute!" She agreed.

Ying updated Amelia on the latest K-Pop songs from her favorite artists and shared her playlist.

"Dinner is ready, girls!" Mrs. Chen called from downstairs. Amelia went and scrubbed her hands before heading downstairs.

While in the bathroom, she admired the white slippers Mrs. Chen gave her to wear when they came in an hour earlier. Amelia didn't know that you couldn't wear shoes inside the house in many Asian countries. She had learned something new and hadn't even been there for that long. She compared her culture and recognized the similarities, like having to leave her shoes at the front door when visiting some relatives and friends of her dad's. She was accustomed to that, although in her household, her parents didn't practice that.

When both girls were ready, they went downstairs and sat at the table next to each other. The Peking duck was steaming on a large, decorated plate, and the aroma of spices and broth floated through the air.

"Have you had duck before?" Ying asked Amelia, who was patiently waiting with hungry eyes.

"No, but it smells delicious, and my stepmom always tells me to always be willing to try foods from other cultures when given a chance to." She shared.

The Chens smiled and agreed with the advice given to her and began cutting pieces of duck and serving the girls. Once each plate was filled with duck and steaming scallion pancakes, everybody dug in.

Amelia took a bite, and the Chens watched and waited for her response. She chuckled and covered her mouth when she realized all of their eyes were on her. She was surprised at how tender the meat was. Lots of meats cooked in Nigeria are much tougher. It was juicy and spicy, with hints of plums and sweetness.

"Wow, this is really good. I like it." She didn't know that duck could be so greasy, but she kept that part to herself.

"Thank you, Amelia. We are so glad that Ying has such kind and respectful friends. So please tell us about Culture Day. How did it go?"

Ying and Amelia spent the first half of dinner talking about culture day, the kids, and the teachers. The other half of dinner was spent listening to Amelia talk about her culture and family while the Chens talked about theirs. The girls learned that although there are many cultures around the globe, many still share similarities.

The Chens found Amelia's jokes funny and understood her sadness when the teachers and classmates didn't try to pronounce her name. Mrs. Chen mentioned the time she remembered when Ying had a really tough time with the same issue. Ying told her parents that Amelia made everyone respect her and call her by her name. She was proud of her friend and truly admired her.

Finally, when dinner was over, the girls got up to pack

Ying's stuff for the night. Once they were in Ying's room, they packed the essentials: pajamas, clothes for the next day, a toothbrush, and anything else she would need for a fun sleepover. When Amelia was in Ying's closet, she saw the prettiest collection of dresses she had ever seen. Amelia took one of them off the rack to admire.

"It's called a Hanfu. It's a traditional Chinese dress for special occasions. You can try it on."

Amelia wasted no time. She loved trying on fancy dresses and playing dress-up. She did so all the time in her mom's closet. She pulled the dress around her and tied it closed. She loved how flowy the dress was. She looked stunning. She walked over to Ying's mirror and pranced around, twisting and turning, and walking an imaginary catwalk. Xiuying squealed and took pictures of her friend. "You look so cute!" Ying squealed. She was always her best friend's hype man—well, hype girl. She put a flower in her hair and became her instant red-carpet photographer. They were having a blast.

After a few minutes of Amelia prancing around in the Hanfu, Mrs. Chen opened the door. She started giving "Oohs and Ahhs." Mrs. Chen could not believe how nice Amelia looked in the Hanfu.

"Wow, Amelia, that looks wonderful on you. Would you like to keep that one? I'm sure Ying wouldn't mind."

"Oh no," Amelia started to say. She thought it wouldn't be right to take her friend's dress. She looked over at Ying, who had cut her off.

"Yes, Amelia!" It's okay to take it. I want you to have it. My gift to you. I have plenty." Ying shook her head, indicating that she wouldn't mind Amelia taking Hanfu home with her. Amelia smiled and agreed to keep it. The Hanfu would look wonderful in Amelia's closet next to all her Nigerian attire.

"I came to get the two of you because your parents are outside waiting."

"Thanks, Mom." "Thanks, Mrs. Chen."

The girls gathered their things and headed to the car with Mr. and Mrs. Chen behind them. As they organized their bags in the back seat, the parents greeted each other.

"Hello, Mr. Ikande, I'm Mr. Chen, and this is my wife." Amelia then introduces Ying to her parents.

"Bawo Ni, Mr. Je," Xiuying nodded her head. "Dad, you're supposed to say Bawo Ni; it means hello," Xiuying said.

The parents chuckled as they shook hands.

"Thank you, Xiuying. Bawo Ni." He greeted the Ikandes again. "And dad, you say, Nǐ hǎo," Amelia said, facing her dad.

The Ikandes greeted the Chens in return. The four of them exchanged first names.

"Wow, you girls are good." Mrs. Ikande and Mrs. Chen chimed in.

"You have a pleasant daughter. I am happy to know that she and my Xiuying have become very good friends."

"Thank you; we appreciate that."

"Alright, girls, are we ready to go?" Amelia's dad asked. "YES!" They sang in unison with excitement.

They climbed into the SUV and said their goodbyes.

"Don't embarrass us, Xiuying," her father joked. The Chens waved them goodbye.

"How was dinner, girls?" Amelia's stepmom asked. "It was delicious. We had Peking Duck."

"Ooh, fancy." She teased, looking back at the girls.

"Since we've already had dinner, can we stop for dessert, please?" Their eyes lit up, hoping for a yes.

Mrs. Ikande's eyes lit up too. She loved ice cream, and

Amelia knew she would say yes.

"Of course!" her dad said.

He threw his arm in the back seat for a couple of fist bumps. "Yes!" "Yes!" was heard from the back seat.

Amelia and Ying were on a high. This week was starting off just right and was going to be the best ever! Dinner was great, and the two couldn't wait to see what the sleepover had in store.

Chapter Six

The Sleepover

The ride was peaceful except for Amelia and Ying chuckling in the backseat over inside jokes and shenanigans that happened at school throughout the week. Oh, and Aiden. Out of nowhere, the quiet ride turned into a party ride when Amelia's stepmom turned on some Afrobeats, and her dad started dancing. Amelia joined in and taught Ying some backseat moves. The whole car was in dance party mode. "Your parents are so much fun," Ying sent a text to Amelia, seated next to her. After a 20-minute ride, they pulled up to Amelia's beautiful 3-story home. It was night, so Ying couldn't fully see all its beauty, but knowing Amelia, it had to be nice. Amelia's father helped the girls get their stuff out of the car, and the 4 of them headed inside the house to meet Amelia's other siblings.

Amelia's stepmom advised the girls to take their things upstairs when they got to the kitchen. The air smelled heavily of spices and garlic. Ying didn't know what was cooking, and although they had just had dinner, she was sure she could make room for a small taste. Amelia walked Ying through the living area, across the study, and into the family room to introduce her to her big sister. Ying looked around and spotted all types of African artifacts and printed fabrics. She remembered that Amelia called them Ankara. There were statues and large framed photographs on the walls of her family here and back home, her home. Ying loved how in touch they were with their culture. Her home was colorful and adorned with Asian art. Still, Amelia's house looked like a museum of African culture to her. They had more cultural stuff than her home.

Amelia's stepmom popped into the family room toward Amelia and Ying to ask if they wanted to taste what was cooking. Ying's eyes lit up with a big yes! Ying learned that her stepmom was very funny and down to earth; it was like Amelia's dad and stepmom were perfect for each other.

Before heading to the kitchen, Amelia introduced her brother and sister. Her sister was older and talked to Ying with a very mature voice, while her brother was the second oldest. He seemed excited to meet Ying and was quite the charmer.

"This is my brother Mitchell and my sister Ava. Guys, this is Xiuying." Amelia made sure to introduce her full name first. "But you can call me Ying," Xiuying said. She reached out to shake Mitchell's hand, but he opted for a fist bump, and she followed the lead. "Nice to meet you, Xiuying." He clapped both hands together and bowed his head. "Ni Hao." The trio of girls laughed with him as he removed himself from their presence. He was definitely showing off for her. Ying was impressed that he got her name right. "Is Mitchell his traditional name?" She asked. "No, it's Sijuwola, and my traditional name is Ayoola." The big sister, too, gave Ying a fist bump. "Wow," she thought out loud. Ying could see that the family was perfect for each other. She could also tell they had lots of fun in that house.

Once all of the introductions were done, Amelia and Ying made their way to the kitchen to taste what was cooking. It was a stew with dried fish and shrimp. On the side was a big pot of Jollof. She remembers Amelia sharing rice with her on a previous lunch day. She liked it, of course, but boy, it was spicy. She quickly guzzled down a bottle of water given to her by Amelia.

Afterward, the girls raced up the stairs to get their sleepover started while Amelia's stepmom fixed some snacks to last them through their fun night.

Amelia's room was so cool. There were lots of pretty colors and decor throughout her room. The closet was packed to the brim with clothes and shoes. It was very evident that they did lots of shopping in this house. She had a big bed, big enough for three or four people, and a big heart pillow with arms sitting on it. "You sleep on the bed alone?" Ying jokingly asked. Ying spun around in a circle momentarily, taking it all in. Amelia stopped her with a chuckle.

"Do you like it?"

Ying began to laugh, too, while she stumbled in circles. She started to get a bit dizzy.

"Like it? I love it!"

She walked over to the gigantic full-length mirror and noticed little note cards sticking out of the frame with writing on them. She read some of them out loud but under her breath.

"I am beautiful."

"I am magical."

"I am brave."

"I can't be stopped."

She read the last one a bit louder. "My name is Oyindasola."

This made Ying smile. Those little self-love notes warmed her. Especially that last one. She remembered how her bestie had checked the whole class, including the teacher!

"I love these."

"Thank you; I made them myself," Amelia responded from her bed. "I say them every morning before I start my day.

Ying's eyes opened wide as she swung around to face her bestie. "I'd like to have some of my own. Can we?" "Of course." Amelia pulled out her craft boxes from under her bed, filled with everything to craft with. Ying now noticed a lot of the pretty decor in Amelia's room she had created herself. The two friends began to unwind. They changed into their pajamas, and Amelia guided Ying on what she used to design her motivation cards. Ying made a few motivational quotes that she liked and added one that said, "I am Xiuying."

She put a Nollywood movie on her tablet and had it ready to play whenever the snacks arrived. In the meantime, Ying insisted that she learn some dance moves so that she would be ready the next time some Afrobeat started playing.

There was a knock at the door, and in walked a big tray of goodies for the movie. They were served with chips, cookies, popcorn, and ice cream. The two got comfy on the king-sized bed and immediately plunged into the snacks. The sound of the movie soon drowned out the sound of the house. The two besties focused intently on the dramatic scene in front of them.

"Is that Nollywood?"

Amelia nodded yes to her stepmom's question. Ying responded before Amelia could.

"Yep, it sure is. I love Nigerian culture. I wish I had learned more about it before now, but I'm glad I finally got the opportunity. I mean the fabrics, the movies, the hair, the accent." She thought it was funny how dramatic Africans talked, with extra emphasis on sounds and words. Honestly, she thought about her own language and how funny the accent sounded in different tones. She'd laugh at her parents and family when they also pronounced words in their thick accents.

Amelia and her stepmom laughed softly at Ying. It was nice to see someone so interested in learning about other cultures. Of course, Amelia's stepmom also shared her interest in the culture.

"Clearly, you can tell I'm not Nigerian, but Amelia's father is. I remember when he was conversing with a friend, and he was so loud and boisterous that I thought he was arguing. Not the case," she laughed. "They just talk very loooud," she exaggerated.

"Yes, I see." Ying laughed along and pointed at the movie.

"Later, girls." She exited the room.

Amelia turned out the lights to make them feel like they were in an actual movie theatre.

Amelia's sister heard everybody congregating in Amelia's room, and she went up the stairs to see all the excitement. She could hear everything her stepmom said, saw the movie playing on the tablet, and couldn't resist. "Hey, is that …? "Both girls turned to her and shook their heads, saying yes. "I love this movie!" Soon it was a group movie fest. Ava climbed onto the bed to watch the movie with them after asking if they'd mind.

As the movie continued, Ying pointed out beautiful braids and hairstyles that she liked on the actresses. There were Bantu knots, box braids, and several other beautiful braided styles. Box braids were her favorite, especially the ones that Amelia had. She pointed out the Bantu knots to Amelia.

"Oh, those are my favorite now. It look-a like-a your haair is a crown. It looks soooo cuute!" Ying mocked her Asian accent with extra dramatics. They all laughed at her dramatics.

"Eh han, yes o! The crown is built into your hair." While demonstrating with her hands, Amelia mocked her Nigerian way of speaking wildly exaggeratedly. Then Ava chimed in.

Ava laughed at the two. She was happy that her sister had met a friend at school. "I could put a couple in if you want." She offered. "I know how to do these styles. The Bantu would look really cool on you." Ying looked at Ava excitedly, and, without wasting any time, she agreed and sat on the floor in front of her as they continued to watch the movie.

By the movie's end, Ying had five beautiful Bantu knots that framed her face from one ear to the other, like a crown.

She even added a few jewels to the knots she would usually add to Amelia's braids. Amelia pulled Ying and rushed her to the mirror to see her new look. "OMG! Look at my crown!" Ying couldn't stop saying, "OMG!"

"Thank you, Ava!"

"Oh my… I look fierce!" She posed in the mirror from one side to the other, admiring the work of Ava.

"I need selfies, Amelia! Where's my phone?!"

She had to have taken about 15 selfies and the other 20 with Amelia. "These are definitely insta-ready," she wasted no time sharing on her social media and tagging Amelia. Ava left the girls for the night to finish their sleepover.

Ying mentioned the end of the year royal nominations for the 8th-grade class. Everyone was talking about it. She fantasized about being the 8th-grade Queen for the year but knew she would never. She was way too shy. She suggested to Amelia that she would be a good match for Queen of the school year.

"Amelia, it would be so cool if you got nominated Princess and won Queen! Imagine the look on Alaina's face when she hears your name called for the winner." Ying was tickled at the thought alone.

"Me? Queen of the school," Amelia laughed. First, we can't nominate ourselves; second, no one would vote for me even if I was nominated. The majority of the 8th-grade barely knows me. I'm still the new girl here, and those who know me still don't like me because of the obvious. I still get mean, dry looks from people walking by. I can't see the girl who came into the 8th grade, middle of the school year, had everyone in an uproar about her name alone, now voting for me to be their Queen for the following school year." Ying just nodded and smiled. Amelia didn't know that Ying had already planned to nominate her. She thought she deserved it and secretly lived through her lively personality.

They finished watching videos from their favorite YouTubers until they could no longer keep their eyes open. Before they knew it, it was 2 am. Ying rolled over to one side of the king-sized bed, Amelia rolled over to the other side, and it was lights out! Right before Amelia drifted off, she heard Ying say something faintly. "Imagine if you and Aiden won King and qu—" Sandman had taken Ying before she could finish her sentence.

Chapter Seven

What Happened?

A couple of weeks later, Amelia walked the halls trying to catch up with Ying when a poster caught her eye. The poster said, "Join Mathletes."

"Ha!" she laughed at the poster. "Who would choose math as a hobby in their free time?" She scrunched her face in disgust. Amelia hated Math, so she wouldn't be joining the Mathletes Club, but that did make her think. Amelia had been at Bridgewater Academy for a couple of months and wasn't involved with anything. She wasn't in any clubs or on any sports teams, and maybe that was something she could look into. She also promised her school counselor that she would scope some clubs out that might pique her interest and at least inquire. Unfortunately, Amelia didn't have much time to think about it at that moment because she was about to be late for her art therapy class.

Actually, Amelia didn't think about it much more for the rest of the day, but on her way out of the building after her last class, she was stopped by the 8th-grade school counselor, Ms. Bardot. Amelia hadn't really spoken to or seen Ms. Bardot much. Still, she knew who she was, as she was one of six teachers and counselors in the whole school with a brown complexion. In other words, she was African American.

"Hi, Ms. Bardot. I'm just heading home for the day."

Ms. Bardot smiled at Amelia, as she did not get the chance to speak to relatively new students every day. And although Oyindasola had been there a few months already, she had only seen her a few times and always made an effort to check in on new students. In addition, Ms. Bardot was one of many who had heard about her first day and how she had set everybody straight when they thought they would tell the new student what was what. She had first heard it from Mr. Grimsky when he mentioned the new girl to her and was baffled at how she objected to his name suggestion for her. Ms. Bardot laughed when he told her that story. She also secretly admired this student and was anxious to meet her then, especially after hearing snippets about her from other students passing by that whole first week.

"Who is this girl?" She'd think to herself. Whoever this girl was had taken the 8th-grade for a loop. So, when she first met Amelia, Ms. Bardot shared with her that she had friends from various African countries, including a couple of them from Nigeria. When she shared her story about how she had thrown the 8th-grade floor into an uproar about getting her name correct, her friends cheered her on. Ms. Bardot's friends loved the story and gave Oyindasola many kudos by way of Ms. Bardot.

"Hey, Amelia, I saw you were looking at the Mathletes poster earlier. I wondered if you were interested in joining. I'm good friends with the teacher, so I could talk to him for you. If you would like to?" Oyindasola laughed. "Ms. Bardot, who does Math for fun? I just can't see it." She shook her head no. Ms. Bardot chuckled and leaned into her.

"Well, you kinda have a good point there." she agreed.

Amelia scoffed at the thought while palming her forehead. "No, thank you!" she finished.

"The designs caught my eye. I like the artwork they added

to suck you in, and then you see the word, 'Math.' I was just reading to see what it said."

Ms. Bardot thought back and didn't recall what activities Amelia did at school.

"Well, have you thought about the Art Club?" I did, but I already have Art Therapy, soooo—" "What activities do you do here? If any—"

Amelia laughed awkwardly and rubbed the back of her neck.

"None. I haven't tried out for anything since I started here so late, and school will be done in just a few months. "

Ms. Bardot didn't like that. She encouraged students to join at least one sport or club. Life and school can be extremely frustrating and stressful, and as she always stressed to them, students require an outlet. She advised Amelia of the necessity of a good emotional outlet.

"Oyindasola, it is really important to have a good emotional outlet. I see the classes you take. You're in advanced English and History while maintaining high Environmental Sciences and Math grades. I know how stressful that could be. When I was your age, I ran track and was a part of Model

United Nations. It allowed me to take the frustrations of my classes much more easily, and it was a much-needed break from constant work and study. I'm not saying you have to do Track or Mathletes, but I encourage you to join something even if school ends in a few months. Some of these clubs continue throughout the summer and carry on to the next school year."

Amelia smiled and promised Ms. Bardot that she would think about it, and she did.

Amelia thought about it all night. What could she be interested in joining? It was time for spring auditions and entries, and there were quite a few things to try out for. She could cheer, debate, or play a sport like soccer. She couldn't decide which one she liked the best, so she just decided to inquire about all of them.

The Spring auditions were scheduled throughout the upcoming week. Though Amelia had to turn down a couple of hangout sessions with Ying, she was pretty much free.

The first auditions were with the cheerleaders. Cheering was really fun. She hadn't thought about Alaina too much since the bathroom event until now. As it turns out, Alaina was trying out as well. She gave Amelia a stare-down before turning her back to her and moving to another section, making sure to keep a few girls between them. Funny enough, she didn't roll her eyes per usual. Amelia acted as if she wasn't there but made a mental note to keep her distance to avoid unnecessary trouble.

First, they warmed up with some stretching; then, they began learning fun chants and catchy rhymes. Amelia had never used pom poms before, but they were definitely the most fun. Plus, she liked the attention cheerleaders got from everyone in the school. Then they worked on some tumbling and flips.

She had perfected her cartwheel in the 3rd grade when her sister said, 'all big girls could do cartwheels.' Amelia was determined to prove that she was no longer a baby.

She tumbled and flipped across the floor with ease. The club sponsors and tryout students watched in surprise and awe. She was really good at this.

By the time tryouts were over, Amelia had secured herself a spot on the Junior Varsity Cheer Squad. She shouted in excitement until she saw the practice schedule. The practice was three days from 3:30 to 5:30, and they had Saturday morning practices. Amelia absolutely could not do that. How would she have time for her homework? Her friends, and even herself? And she knew her father would disapprove of her spending more time jumping around and dancing than schoolwork. It would be too much for her, so she was back trying out for another club the next day.

The next day, there was an info session for the Debate team. Again, Amelia showed up, ready to argue. Everyone always said she would make a great lawyer because she constantly had rebuttals for accusations or argued when things weren't going her way. Oh yeah, and she talked a lot. This would be a piece of cake for her.

She walked in, signed up, and sat down. She saw that Imani and Aaliyah were there and sat next to them.

The trio chatted and caught up since they first met in the hall over a month ago. They didn't see each other often because they all had different schedules and took classes at various levels, but there were only a few brown girls in the 8th grade, so they were always able to spot each other and always waved and smiled from a distance.

The girls saw her coming in their direction and started throwing punches in the air. Amelia caught on and laughed at their joke. As it turns out, Natalia told them about the bathroom event, and Imani responded with, "I got your back."

Everything moved so slowly. The debate team was facilitated by one of the Humanities instructors. He explained what the club was about, their roles, and the benefits of debating. They started with small breakout groups and did a mock session so everyone could understand how things would flow. He gave each group a topic and then gave each member a position. Then they had to gather evidence and pick a side to argue. Then, they had to argue. It was slow and super repetitive. By the end, all Amelia wanted to do was curl up and take a nap. She decided that debate definitely was not for her, no matter that it only met once a week for two hours. The task of it all was just exhausting.

Lastly, it was soccer tryouts. This was Amelia's last shot. After that, if soccer didn't work, she would accept her fate and not do any sports or clubs. But, at least, she could honestly tell Ms. Bardot that she had tried as promised.

Amelia walked onto the field in her gym attire and tied her

sneakers. She played back in Nigeria, where it's called "football." The athletics teacher blew the whistle and called all the girls to the line. The girls then made sprints, passing, and shooting drills for over an hour. Amelia did it with a bit of trouble. It was way too hot for her and showed her speed and shot accuracy. She was one of the better soccer players on the field but by no means the best. After an hour and a half of tryouts, the coach announced the teammates. Amelia and the other students waited and waited while the coach announced the varsity players. Those were the 9th graders. The 8th graders got junior varsity.

She couldn't believe that she had worked so hard in the heat. Yes, it was Spring, but the sun was out and was on everybody's back.

Then the coach got to Junior Varsity. Amelia's name was the first to be called.

"Oyindasola, You're Jersey Number 1. Here you go."

She was on the team!

"Ehh! Me? Oyin-da-sola? Numba' one?" She added emphasis to her accent. Of course, she got some eye rolls from a few other girls because of it. Some still disliked her because of her first day's antics. They just couldn't let it go. But most of the other mates, including the coach, laughed with her. They knew it was all in good fun.

The coach tossed Amelia her jersey and continued down the JV roster. When everyone who made either team's name was called, the coach passed out training schedules. Amelia prayed they were better than the cheerleaders were. She knew she would definitely get her father's approval for soccer.

JV practices twice weekly, from 3:30 to 4:45 p.m., with no weekends. Amelia could agree to this. She could have her extracurriculars and still have a life.

Amelia picked up her stuff and pumped her fist as she and some teammates she met from the team walked back into the building to wait for their rides. She saw Ying at her locker and stopped for a second. "Hey Ying, what's up?"

Ying turned around and watched the group of girls that Amelia was walking with continuing down the hall. Ying could feel her stomach tighten with jealousy. How could Amelia blow her off, her best friend, to hang out with someone else?

"I'm fine." She shrugged her shoulders. Her Bantu knots

had fallen, and her hair was pulled back into its usual low ponytail.

Ying slammed her locker shut and shuffled herself down the hall in the opposite direction. Amelia stood there stunned for a couple moments before concluding that Ying was just having a bad day. She went the way her teammates went, hoping to catch up with them before they left. That itself turned Ying's slight jealousy into serious envy. Her bestie didn't know it, but Ying's feelings were hurt.

Chapter Eight

And the Nominees Are–

Amelia called and texted Ying for days without a response. Text after text, she was left on 'read.' She didn't understand what was going on. What did she do wrong? Finally, when Amelia and Ying were in class, Ying sat on the opposite side of the room and tried her best not to talk or even look in Amelia's direction. Although Amelia caught her side-eyeing a few times, she was still left wondering.

Amelia didn't know what to do or why Ying wouldn't talk to her. The school would soon end for the summer. So many activities were happening that it felt lonely not to have to make plans and have fun with her, especially since the 8th-grade dance was right around the corner. That was the biggest end-of-the-year event.

They had plans to go together, of course, and they could

not stop talking about it since the posters went up in the halls. And although Amelia now had other friends to go with, it wouldn't be the same without her "bestie."

She had an idea a few times that maybe Ying was jealous when she saw her with other students, like when she had first seen her with Aaliyah, Jada, and Imani. The only other girls she hung out with were the few from the soccer team, and they really were only together when it was time to head to or leave practice. She even recalled suggesting Ying join Soccer with her, but she didn't want to. Ying just wasn't interested in any of the suggestions she made.

Over time, Amelia noticed that in private, Ying was lively, but around crowds, she was quiet and reserved, almost a bit shy sometimes, so it made sense why she didn't want to join the Cheer team, Soccer, or Debate. Honestly, had they joined a mutual club, that would have allowed them to hang out more and do homework together. It would have made Amelia's busy schedule a bit more bearable since that would have crossed off two things off her list. She would have her homework done, and her social life would have already been built in. The one club that Ying did join, Amelia just couldn't bring herself to join with her. She just couldn't. There was no way she could bring herself to join Mathletics. She also knew that just like she had made new friends with her team, Ying surely had to have made friends in her Math Club, so she wouldn't be lonely there. Besides, who else will they talk to about Math besides each other?

Now, the issue was that the Soccer team and Mathletics had met on different days, which meant when Ying was meeting, Amelia was free, and when Amelia was meeting, Ying was free. Their schedules just didn't match. Once Ying started ghosting her, she started spending more time with them.

Amelia wanted a new dress for the dance, and her parents agreed. She and Ying had made plans to go together, of course, but Ying still hadn't talked to her. So when Char mentioned that she should accompany her, Reece, and Andi, she still really wanted to go with Ying, but she always had fun with her teammates.

Andi was the JV team captain and an absolute Math whiz. There was no goal she couldn't score or a Math problem she couldn't solve. She knew that she and Ying would get along really well. Andi wanted to join the Math Club, but she loved

Soccer more. She was even taking 9th-grade Math courses on the 9th-grade floor. There was Charlotte, or Char for short. She was the self-proclaimed beauty Queen of the team. She had shoulder-length dark curly hair and always carried her book bag full of makeup. Char and Amelia had lots in common. They were both into glam. She was so funny and sweet. She played midfield on the JV soccer team.

Then there was Reece. Reece was a tomboy with a love for all things sports, but she still got her manicures and pedicures and occasionally wore lip gloss, but it had to be clear. She played all the sports all year round. She was JV's goalie, and an awesome one at that. She was always there to lend a hand or make a joke about Char and her bag of face paint. Together, along with Amelia, they had become close ever since tryouts.

So, the following Saturday, all four girls met at the front of the mall with their moms. Amelia didn't really know what she wanted. Her dress closet had an array of styles, so she hoped to find something new and different. She wanted something pretty and bold but not too sparkly, but definitely some sparkle. Her stepmom had given her $200 to shop with. The girls begged their moms to let them shop alone and promised to be on their best behavior and to only come back with what they were supposed to buy. Amelia's stepmom reminded her that she still had to look like a young lady, whatever dress she chose. Judging by the head nods and looks on the other moms' faces, that rule also applied to their daughters. "Okay," they all agreed in unison before walking away.

The girls rushed into every store that displayed party dresses and touched almost every dress in the shops. They pulled out dress after dress. Of course, Reece pulled some suits, but they still added a touch of femininity without overdoing it and being too girly. There was no way she would be caught dead in one of those glittery monstrosities.

Together, they took on the dressing rooms and tackled dress after dress. Sometimes they switched dresses; other times, the dresses immediately went into the 'no thank you' pile. Amelia and Char twirled in the mirrors while Andi and Reece took mirror photos of them all. They were clearly having a lot of fun. Finally, Amelia ran from the back dressing rooms to pick up another handful of dresses. She hadn't even taken off the dress she had tried on last. Char followed to give her a hand. Amelia grabbed another arm full of dresses before accidentally dropping one over her shoulder. She turned around to pick it up, and on the other side of the shopping plaza's courtyard stood Ying and her mom. Ying looked at her from across the courtyard with shopping bags in her hand.

They locked eyes for what felt like an eternity. Amelia could do nothing but stare at her. The two were probably thinking the same thing. "There goes, my best friend." Several cars stopped at the stop sign, breaking their line of vision, and when the cars pulled off, Ying's mother's car had also pulled out of its parking spot with Ying still looking at her through the back seat window. "Why didn't she wave? Why didn't I wave? What is happening to us?" she questioned herself. Char saw Amelia in a frozen state and stared out the window.

"You alright?"

Amelia turned her head away from Char to hide the sadness on her face, but she couldn't hide it in her demeanor.

"Yeah, I'm fine. Let's take these back to the others." Her energy has shifted a bit.

And so they did.

Amelia found a dress she loved, and everyone else found something that suited their personalities and style.

Now, two weeks later was the dance. It was all the 8th-graders could talk about. Who was going with whom? Who was going to be the 8th-grade King and Queen? And what was everybody wearing? But, of course, Amelia and her teammates weren't exempt from this excitement, and even with how excited Amelia was, she missed her best friend. She wished she knew why Ying was mad at her and what she could do to fix it.

It was Monday at lunch, and everybody was on the edge of their seats, waiting for the announcement of the nominations. While everyone focused on waiting for the announcements, Char took the opportunity to ask Amelia about what had happened with her in the dress shop window. She noticed her saddened face then but didn't want to pry immediately. Char listened intently as Amelia gave her a short synopsis of what went down. She didn't speculate much, but she did offer Amelia some words. "Don't worry; she probably feels like you replaced her. I think you should keep trying to talk to her. She will come around eventually and see that it's not what she thinks. Invite her to sit with us. There's always room for one more." Char had experienced this first-hand just last summer, but with a cousin. She simply shared the advice that was given to her. "Thanks, Char."

They leaned in and bumped shoulders.

The 8th-grade Princes and Princesses were ready to be announced. The nominees had to be nominated by someone other than themselves, including why they should be in the royal court. The girls clutched each other's hands, and the guys rolled their eyes at the girls' antics. Truth be told, they were just as excited, but you know how cool guys try to act. Almost everyone wanted to hear their names called. Suddenly, the intercom in the 8th-grade lunchroom came on.

"Hello, everyone, and good afternoon. This is your Principal, Mrs. Allen, here. I know you are all extremely excited to hear about this year's 8th-grade Princes and Princesses nominees. Being nominated by your peers is a huge honor. Out of all the nominees, the academy's counselors have narrowed it down. We looked for those who reflect the values and characteristics this school is looking for." There were some "oohs and awes" in the crowd. Unfortunately, those few knew they were already out of the running.

"It is an honor to announce the four Princes and Princesses every year, as this seems to be the highlight of the school year's closing.

'Come on already, Mrs. Allen!'"

A dozen students could be heard being impatient and complaining about her long speech. It felt like torture. She was dragging it out on purpose. This is one of the few times she would have the full attention of the entire floor at once.

"Now, without further ado, this year's royal court consists of—by the way; what's for lunch today?"

"Nooo," they pleaded. Of course, they knew exactly what she was doing. Some of the students grew more impatient, as if their lives were in limbo, and others laughed at her antics.

"I think I will stop in and grab a sandwich. Somebody save me a seat, please." She released a hearty laugh from the speaker. She was having fun at their expense.

Although she was in her office, she was only down the hall and could hear all the uproar she was causing.

"Come on, Mrs. Allen, stop torturing us!"

"Alright, alright, alright," she started. The Prince nominees are as follows: Jersey Williams, Shane Durvy, Andres Martin, and Jaleel Thurgood. Congrats, gentlemen, and good luck on winning the crown."

The lunchroom sounded off with a round of congratulatory applause while the boys played it cool, popped their collars, and waved like they were presidents.

"Alright, ladies, and now for our Princesses. The nominees are Danita Reno, Charla Grant, Lelani Woods, and Oyindasola Ikande!"

Another round of congratulatory applause filled the room. The girls did not play it as cool. They didn't play it cool at all. There were screams and jumps of joy all throughout the lunchroom. Amelia's eyes grew big as she was shocked to hear her name. She heard a few faint 'boos' following her name, but she didn't care. She was more concerned with how did she get nominated and by whom? Char and Amelia high-fived each other in all the excitement because they had both been nominated.

"Thank you so much, students, for nominating your contestants. Young men and young ladies, thank you for being good examples to your peers. Don't forget to cast your votes for King and Queen by this Friday at the end of the day. You may only vote once. Enjoy the rest of your day."

The noise level was almost deafening as soon as the loudspeaker was cut off. It was so loud that the teachers opted to step into the hallway and let them enjoy the moment before quieting them down soon enough.

Alaina was seen leaving the lunchroom with a not-so-happy look on her face. Her name clearly wasn't called for a nomination. Cheerleading and being 8th-grade Queen were her main interest at Bridgewater. Unfortunately, this year, she didn't make either of them.

Excitement, anger, confusion, and a hundred other emotions were going around the room. Amelia was in shock. She? An 8th-grade Princess and maybe even a Queen? She went from the most hated person in the grade to one of the favorites in a matter of months. Amelia couldn't believe it, but she was happy, nonetheless. She immediately texted her sister the news.

Andi and Reece, and the rest of the soccer team gathered around Amelia and Char to cheer and congratulate their teammates. Amelia felt a tap on her right shoulder when a voice behind her said, "Congratulations, Amelia. I know you're going to win, Queen."

She turned her head, recognizing the voice, to see that it was a smiling Aiden, as she expected. She smiled back.

"Thanks, Aiden."

"Is it okay if we meet up at the dance?" He asked.

His hands nervously tapped on his legs as he waited for her response.

"Yeah, okay. That would be cool."

"Okay, see you then." He walked off to rejoin his friends.

"Somebody has a date; somebody has a daaaate!" The girls quietly sang in a teasing tone.

Amelia didn't say a word. She just shook her head no. This had to be the second-best lunch she's had this school year. She is a nominated Princess and now has a date, kinda, and all in one day. "Oh, I wish Ying was here," she thought. Amelia was so excited she couldn't focus for the rest of the afternoon. Even her favorite class, Art Therapy, was a bit of a blur. Who nominated her for the 8th-grade Princess? It could have only been a handful of people. A member of her soccer team... Aiden was a possibility. He seemed to have taken a liking to her, and it showed. Then it hit her, and she gasped, and her eyes widened. Ying! She remembered Ying slurred something about being prom Queen at their sleepover. Yes! It had to be Ying!

Once she calmed herself, she immediately responded to her sister's message and updated her with the details.

Chapter Nine

Diamonds & Pearls

F inally, today was the day. It was the evening of the 8th-grade dance. The academy had three grade levels: grades 7, 8, and 9. Each grade had an entire floor and its own lunchroom. The 7th graders had their dance a week prior, and the 9th graders would have theirs next week. Amelia had heard the 9th graders raving about last year's dance party and the 7th graders raving about last week's party, so she was ready for this.

Amelia slipped into her dress while her stepmom zipped it up. Amelia looked at herself in the mirror with much admiration. She has dressed up plenty of times for plenty of events, but that was with her family; this one was different. Amelia was happy and nervous at the same time. Happy that she was Princess but nervous that she may not win. Anyway, she thought, *"Hey, I got nominated."* She twirled about a dozen times in her full-length mirror to get her dress to twirl. She thought back on all the other dresses she had tried on and was still pleased with her choice.

She chose a knee-length sleeveless blush pink party dress with a sequin bodice and silver kitten heels to match the sparkles. Her hair was slicked up into a big dramatic afro puff with a sequin bow at the back of it to match the dress and shoes. Her eyes crept up her body from her toes to her hair, ensuring everything was in place. For just a moment, she was tickled; she wondered what Aiden would think when he saw her.

A pair of sparkly stud earrings sat comfortably in her ears to finish the look. It was perfect for Amelia. Ava had done Amelia's makeup in a very beautiful yet natural way. She only wore mascara and very light eyeshadow to match her dress and lip gloss to finish the look.

Amelia couldn't describe how beautiful she felt, yet even when she felt her most beautiful, she also felt her most sad. No matter the moment or event, she still missed her bestie. It had been nearly three weeks, going on 4, without a word from

Ying. Frankly, it was affecting Amelia more than she wanted to admit. Amelia sighed and kept a smile for her family before grabbing her purse and going downstairs to take pictures. They knew nothing about what was happening between the two, and she wanted to keep it that way. The less she talked about it, the less she had to talk about it.

Downstairs, her father was camera ready as usual. He was always ready to snap photos when events arose. As soon as she hit the middle step—"Ooh, look at you, my little baby," he grinned ear to ear.

He snapped her pictures one after the other, from the middle of the staircase all the way to the front door.

"You're a fine, fine girl." He continued the compliments.

"You look just like your daddy!" He boasted. "Thank you, da-ddy." She smiled.

"Who picked out this dress?" He asked.

"I did!" she exclaimed as she spun around. "Beautiful! You look like a young lady." "Thank you!"

Amelia received compliments from her family, and she soaked it all up! Shion grabbed the camera out of her husband's hand so she could get out of the door on time.

Photo after photo. Silly pose, serious pose, cute pose, until Amelia knew that the camera's storage must be filled to maximum capacity. She didn't mind. She loved taking photos, and she was used to his antics. Grabbing her small silver wristlet bag, she headed outside. Once outside, Amelia looked around the driveway and up and down the street. What was she looking for?

"Da-ddy, where is my carriage? Haven't you heard? I am the Princess of Bridgewater," she teased.

"Un-han, my Princess, your chariot has arrived." He bowed his head and waved his hand towards the backseat of his black SUV when he opened the door for her. The family got a good laugh from that one.

"I didn't know Lexus made chariots." His wife chimed in.

"Yes! It's the new-new. It's a limited edition. Only a few can get it. We are a very fortunate family."

They laughed again. They always got a good laugh with each other. Amelia's chauffeur, a.k.a. dad, seated her in the chariot and drove her to the dance.

Amelia wondered if Ying would be there. What would she be wearing? Would they show up in the same color? Were they even going to finally talk? She ruled out being sad for the night. This would be a great night regardless of what was happening. She would handle Ying when the time came. She had decided that if she saw Ying tonight, they would end whatever the issue was, and if she wasn't there, she would pay Ying a surprise visit at home the next day. Enough was enough! Amelia and Char met up outside to walk in together.

There was a red carpet with lights shining down on it, and the music was so loud you could hear it before reaching the door. The girls took photos from every angle on that red carpet. Her dad wished he had brought his camera with him. Once inside, they met up with Reece and Andi and found a table. Every time the door opened, Amelia's neck would snap, wondering if Ying would be coming through it. They danced and took selfies non-stop.

The gym was full of students, and everyone looked good. The photographer came around, and the girls instantly became models and posed together as if they were shooting for an album cover. Then, they went to the dance floor and began to party with the other students. Aiden found Amelia, and his eyes lit up when he saw her. He thought she looked so beautiful. He just looked at her and said, "Wow!" She blushed in acceptance of his compliment. She admired his looks too. She looked at him from head to toe and gave him a nod of approval. He brushed off his shoulders and nodded back.

"Can I dance with you?" She looked at her girls, not wanting to blow them off for a boy, but they egged her on to dance with him. So she did. Soon his friends came over, and they all danced as a group. The night was filled with lots of energy. The lights were low, spotlights were flowing through the crowd, the DJ played all the right music and kept the crowd moving, and there was plenty of food and drinks. Bridgewater knew how to throw a party. There were all types of music; some didn't even go together. First, there was country music, then line dancing, then rap. He played something for everybody. The girls didn't care what was playing; they continued to dance and have fun regardless of whether they liked or knew the song.

Amelia even stepped away for a bit when she saw Jada, Aaliyah, and Imani. She didn't get to see them often and used this time to hang out with everyone she had met that was nice to her since she had started there. She even chatted with and took selfies with Natalia for a brief moment.

Amelia didn't know yet, but yes, Ying was there. She sat with a few of her Math Club mates and had been watching her the entire time. Ying started to realize that Amelia was allowed to have other friends as she did, that, of course, she would meet new people if she joined school clubs, and no, it wouldn't change the fact that they were best friends. Amelia didn't push her away; Ying left. That night, she saw Amelia partying with everybody. She covered her mouth and smiled when she saw her dancing with Aiden. She was missing Amelia as much as she was being missed.

Amelia partied the evening away, dancing with everyone until it was time to finally announce the 8th-grade King and Queen when she rejoined her soccer mates. The Principal, Mrs. Allen, and Vice Principal, Mr. Broden, walked to the stage and motioned for the DJ to cut the music. The DJ paused the music, and Principal Allen commended the students for a good year and went on and on about something that became a blur to Amelia. She took a moment to peer around the large room again, looking for Ying. Principal Manning cleared his throat to speak, and it caught her attention.

"Hello, students. When I look around this room, I see the culmination of months of hard work. Students, please give a round of applause to everyone who made this event happen. From the PTA to your counselors, a.k.a. party squad, to the DJ, and, of course, your hosts with the most, Principal Allen and Vice Principal Broden. We all worked tirelessly to make this dance perfect for you guys."

The whole room went up in applause and cheers, but the entire room was waiting for the most important evening announcement, and this was Bridgewater's 8th-grade King and Queen. Principal Allen started. "I know that you are all very excited about this year's 8th-grade King and Queen. This year's runners-up were extremely close, and I, along with every one of you, know how deserving each and every one of our 8th-grade nominees is of this honor. This means that the winners will be King and Queen for the upcoming 9th-grade school year. Let's start with the King, Mr. Broden." She passed the mic.

This Prince has consistently demonstrated leadership and is a team player for his peers. He tutors his peers when needed and always encourages those who need it.

This year's 8th-grade King is Jaleel Thurgood!"

Jaleel, or Ja as everyone called him, made his way up to the stage and was crowned while the room applauded, hooped, and hollered for him.

"Would you like to say something?" Mr. Broden gave him the mic.

Ja's smile reached from ear to ear.

"Thanks, guys; I appreciate this." He passed the mic back.

"A man of many talents and a man of little words," he joked. The crowd laughed at the joke and applauded again.

"And now for the ladies." He passed the mic to Mrs. Allen and stepped to the side.

"Hey, Ladiiies!" Mrs. Allen sang into the mic, then held it out to the crowd, and all the girls screamed out.

"Alright, we are in the building. This Queen is kind but also stands up for herself and teaches others to do so.

She's fun and inspiring but knows when to draw boundaries and is compassionate. So, without further waiting, I would like to introduce this year's 8th-grade Queen; Ms. Oyindasola—!" Principal Allen couldn't even get her last name out before the entire 8th-grade went into a roar of screams, applause, hoop, and hollers for Amelia. Amelia had to fight back her tears of happiness. Her eyes widened, her mouth hung wide in disbelief, and her body froze. She could not believe what she had just heard. She took a few deep breaths. She went from being hated to loved in just a few months.

"Me?" she questioned, clutching her chest as if she couldn't breathe.

Reece and Aiden pushed her toward the stage because she couldn't move.

"Get up here, girl, come get this crown!" Principal Allen exclaimed with laughter.

Amelia finally snapped out of it, and Ja grabbed her hand and pulled her up the steps. Amelia looked at the crowd, still cheering for her when she got on the stage. Even Mr. Grimsky had a slight smile on his face. She looked from left to right. Amelia looked into the eyes of every single person who was clapping and cheering for her. It was like time moved in slow motion. Principal Allen placed a crown around her afro puff. As Amelia's eyes finally got to the right side of the room, her eyes locked with someone else's. It was Ying, standing in a chair so she could see the stage, and she wore the biggest smile on her face. Ying wore a soft yellow halter dress with a pearl studded belt and yellow strappy sandals. Her ears wore pearl studs to match her belt, and her hair was in a half-up, half-down bun. Yellow was definitely her color.

Principal Broden gave her the mic for a speech. "I know you have something you want to say," he joked. Amelia grabbed the mic and held it with both hands. She took a deep breath before she spoke. The room went silent.

"I definitely was not expecting this. I went from not being liked to now having all of this. I just want to quickly say, always be your authentic self, always stand up for yourself, and always remember who you are. Thank you to everyone who voted for me, and lastly, a big warm thank you to the person who nominated me. You are just as amazing as you think I am." Her eyes shot over to where Ying was standing in the chair, but she was no longer there. She passed the mic back to Principal Allen, who asked the crowd to give another round of applause for the King and Queen.

Students erupted in another round of cheers for the two winners, as instructed. The two locked hands took a bow and posed for photos together before exiting the stage. The

DJ turned the music back up, and the party was back in full effect. Amelia walked down the steps of the stage and through the crowd. People moved and went to congratulate her, but Amelia's focus was on another place. Finally, they met. Ying was waiting at the end of the stage entrance and immediately reached out her arms and wrapped them around Amelia.

"Ma binu," she whispered in her ear.

Amelia didn't know what had caused the rift in her and Ying's friendship, and she didn't quite care at that moment. She would probably never bring it up unless Ying did first. So she embraced her right back.

"Ma bin," Amelia responded.

She missed them finishing each other's sentences, sharing food from home, and having each other's backs when someone stepped out of line and sharing their crazy photos on social media. They partied the rest of the evening together and did what they did best: laughed, filled up their phones with photos, and shared them on social media.

"Thank you for nominating me. I love you for this!"

"You deserve it!'

"Wait a minute," Amelia paused. "Where did you learn Ma binu from?"

Ying shrugged her shoulders and smiled. Aiden and his friends joined them. They all congratulated Amelia again and enjoyed the party together. Char saw Amelia from the other side of the room and waved, then gave her a thumbs up. This made Amelia smile. The photographer came around once more to snap her picture with Ying and appropriately hash tagged it #DiamondsAndPearls. Then they all took a group photo.

This night was ethereal, and she didn't want it to end. Amelia made her way to the DJ table and put in a request. Minutes later, the beat dropped, and over the speakers, the DJ said, "Hey Ying, this one's for you girl!"

Ying looked up in shock when she heard her name. He put on some Afrobeats, and Amelia pulled Ying up to dance. This definitely made her night. She had never smiled so hard.

"Hi, orukọ

mi ni"

Poetry

for the culture

My Name Is

A poem about name appreciation

Hi, my name is…

Not to be misused

Shortened for anyone's ease

My name is…

Kin to culture

Close to heart

It isn't anxious or eager to please

Hi, my name is…

Filled to the brim with spirit

Not complicated, odd, or outdated

It's music to the ears when you hear it

My name is…

Letters and sights and sounds

Not a problem to fix

Or lost to be found

My name is…

Full, even, and complete

My body, my hands, and my feet

It is heart, healing, and soul

Never too difficult or old

Hi, my name is…

Black and bold

Good as gold

African heritage it holds

My name is…

Meant to be said in wonder

Bursting with light and full of color

My name is lightning chasing thunder

Hi, my name is…

Unique and flawlessly free

My name is…

Perfectly good for me

Love Your Skin

A poem about authentically loving yourself
for who you are

A love like this we seek,
an admiration in this way we find.
Nothing short of a mountain's peak.
Nothing less than infinite time.

Good sweet sun,
better warmth in the soul within.
Beautiful, bountiful, bursting color,
a deep and fruitful skin.

You are beautiful in every way.
Truly meant to be admired.
A love of culture unlike any other.
Like heat on the edges of fire.

We are sunlight on open water.
A turn in the ocean's waves.
Individual and unique,
no skin will ever look the same.

A canvas blessed by the heavens,
a sky we reach for from above.
Something wonderful, what a marvel,
a skin so worthy of love.

Golden thing, may you never forget.
Sunflower, may you always know.
For wherever you venture in this life,
wherever you might go.

The truth is buried deep within you,
the places it rests on your heart.
Remember you are fully
and wholly beautiful,
an incredible work of art.

A Tale of Two Friends

A poem about friendship appreciation

Moon and sun
Day and night
Morning and evening
Darkness and light

Both rather beautiful
But neither one the same
They may see eye to eye sometimes
But they differ in claims to fame

One draws the horizon out of its shell
And warms the earth below it
The other realizes the night needs light
And decides on its own to bestow it

One is ready for the dawn and the dusk
Another for a quiet midnight

As one of them rises, the other sets
Neither rhythm puts up a fight

Two cultures, two colors,
Two ways of being
Two sides of one whole string
Two shades ever-lovely in their prime
What light their shining brings

Finding harmony within each other
Loving the differences in one another

A friend in the way of the world
The most gifted and different girls

This Is Me

A poem about Self-Love and Appreciation

You know, it's not nice to tell someone that they're not pretty.

So, why am I taught to tell that to myself? It's truly a pity.

It's been said so much that I have to come up with witty ways to defeat those voices that make me feel guilty.

And they're loud. So loud that I hear them from here to Mississippi.

They tell me that my skin is too dark because it's not like the ones on tv.

My nose is too wide and my lips are too big to be fun. But have you seen my skin when it's hit by the sun?

An armor of gold, it becomes.

My cute nose sits above my beautiful lips on my perfect face.

And they suit me. They make me myself.

I love every part of myself no matter what you say.

Questions for Group Discussion

1. What did you think about the main character, Oyindasola?

2. Is your name uncommon? How do you handle others when they say it wrong? Do you correct them?

3. What do you know about your name? It's origin?

4. Were you able to relate to Oyindasola? If yes, did she inspire you?

5. What is the significance of the title? Did you find it meaningful, why, or why not?

6. What did you like most and least about the story?

7. Are there any books that you would compare this to?

8. What did you take away (learn) from this story?

9. What scene would you point out as the pivotal moment in the narrative? How did it make you feel?

10. Which was your favorite chapter and why?

11. How did you feel about the ending? How might you change it?

12. What do you think will happen next to the main characters?

13. Have any of your personal views changed because of this story? If so, how?

14. Which poem do you like most?

15. If you could talk to the author, what question would you want to ask?

Coming Soon!

<u>Children</u>

Brayden's Bedtime Adventures

Sina's Bedtime Adventures

Detective Brayden *(In the Case of the Missing Chocolate Chip Cookies)*

Brayden for President

<u>Tween & Young Adult</u>

The Cupcake in the Window

An Angel in the East Wing

Of the Moon and the Stars

Made in the USA
Middletown, DE
03 December 2022

16447651R00086